MW01137402

One who is loved

Jennifer Taylor

authorHOUSE®

Tracy,

Thanks for your support. Wishing you all the best!

Jenifer

AuthorHouse™
1663 Liberty Drive
Bloomington, IN 47403
www.authorhouse.com
Phone: 1 (800) 839-8640

© *2016 Jennifer Taylor. All rights reserved.*

No part of this book may be reproduced, stored in a retrieval system, or transmitted by any means without the written permission of the author.

Published by AuthorHouse   08/07/2019

ISBN: 978-1-5246-5048-3 (sc)
ISBN: 978-1-5246-5047-6 (e)

Print information available on the last page.

Any people depicted in stock imagery provided by Thinkstock are models, and such images are being used for illustrative purposes only.
Certain stock imagery © Thinkstock.

This book is printed on acid-free paper.

Because of the dynamic nature of the Internet, any web addresses or links contained in this book may have changed since publication and may no longer be valid. The views expressed in this work are solely those of the author and do not necessarily reflect the views of the publisher, and the publisher hereby disclaims any responsibility for them.

Acknowledgement

First, giving all the honor to God!

To my children… God blessed me with a boy and a girl in that order. You both add meaning to my life and are the reasons I shine. I love and cherish you both for the amazing individuals you are.

To my Father and Mother… Thanks for nurturing my heart… I love you both beyond the stars!

To my sister… Thanks for understanding me like no other. I love you to the moon and back!

To my brothers… each of you add a special meaning to my life… nothing like encouraging words of a brother. I love each of you beyond the ocean!

To my nephews and nieces… I love you all for keeping me young. You all rock in your own special way and I love each of you as tall as the tallest of trees!

My family is big with beautiful hearts… I would be remiss to leave out a host of cousins, aunts, and uncles. You all add to my experience and I love you all more than I can put in words!

To my amazing friends both far and near, words cannot express the meaning you add to my life. You know who you are… I love you all!

CHAPTER 1

The Promise

The overly repetitive white and blue tile of the university hospital ended as I reached the end of the hallway. Left standing under the fluorescent lighting and in front of the pale blue doors, I was forced to think of all that happened. Loose strings of conversations that meant so much at the time were now buried alongside the memory of a close childhood friend. It's strange how so much and so little can change all at once. "Man, those bricks were hot," I remember Pookie saying as we reminisced about those hot summer nights wasted on the porches of 9th Avenue. Those porches, that sky, they all seemed worlds away from the realities I face now.

In Pookie's fading eyes I saw a smile as I promised that I would help Latonja get settled into a life without him. I only had to figure out an approach, as I had been absent from her life as long as I had been absent from Pookie's life.

THE APPROACH

Breaking her silence, Latonja introduced her sons to Terrance. She watched Terrance's reaction as she introduced each of her sons, looking for an inkling of criticism. Standing in a corner with her arms folded and searching for a glimmer of the Terrance she once knew, she watched as he interacted with each of them. Kneeling to say hello to the youngest of her

1

sons, Terrance looked over at Latonja for a moment and then smiled as the boy pulled away to join his brothers.

"Thanks for coming over, Latonja. Mama was happy when I told her you were coming over today with your children."

Latonja, wearing a low-cut blouse with tight jeans and 4inch heels, placed her oversized purse on the coffee table and sat down on the edge of the sofa crossing her legs and folding her arms.

"The boys were happy too. They like your Mama."

Terrance could see that Latonja was uncomfortable and worried that she would notice that he too was uncomfortable and trying not to stare at her cleavage.

"Do you want something to drink or eat?"

"Nah, we ate before we came over here."

Latonja uncrossing her legs leaned forward.

"Terrance, I appreciate you trying to help, but I can handle things you know."

"I'm sure you can Latonja, and I don't think Pookie thought you could not. He left us trusting in my expertise as an attorney. I would love to just point you in the right direction if nothing more, if you don't mind."

"I don't, but how are you going to do that?"

Latonja more relaxed leaned back resting her back against the sofa.

"I'm glad you asked. I have printed information and pictures of a couple of homes that are available for rent and a few cars for you to look at."

Terrance reached over the coffee table to hand the papers to Latonja.

"I think you would be off to a good start if you could move to a better neighborhood and had your own transportation."

With raised eyesbrows and a frown on her face, Latonja reached for the papers.

"What's wrong with my neighborhood?"

"Come on Latonja, you know I didn't mean anything by that. I grew up there. Let me re-phrase my comment. A different neighborhood will offer better schools for your sons."

"If you say so."

Terrance stood up and walked over to the mantle with both hands on his head as if he was trying to think of another way to reach Latonja without offending her.

"Chill Terrance, I get what you are saying. I was just messing with you."

A sigh of release, Terrance sat back in the chair and watched as Latonja looked over the information he had given to her.

After a couple of hours of looking over the pictures and information, Latonja chose the house and car she wanted. Terrance made the phone calls.

To both Terrance and Latonja's surprise, things moved faster than expected. Latonja purchased a black Toyota Camry and was able to move into the rental home she picked within a couple of days.

With mixed emotions about the start of her life in a new place, Latonja knew she had to move forward as Pookie had requested. She registered her children in their new school. She purchased furniture for her new home and a computer for her sons.

Two days before Terrance was scheduled to go back to New York, he phoned Latonja to ask if he could take her and her sons out to dinner before he left town.

Latonja was more comfortable around Terrance now that she had spent some time with him but not to the point where she wanted to have dinner with him. She felt it would be awkward for her and her children. In her own special way, she declined the dinner offer.

"You can take me and the boys to the park." she offered instead.

"Sounds good. I'll pick you all up tomorrow around six."

Terrance wanted to have a conversation with Latonja about her future now that she was settled.

It didn't matter to him whether it was over dinner or at a park.

The next day, Terrance arrived to pick up Latonja and her sons.

Pausing before ringing the doorbell, he noticed all the children playing in the neighborhood, the manicured lawns, and the trees surrounding each of the homes. He found comfort in knowing Latonja and her children were living in a safer neighborhood. He smiled and turned back to ring the doorbell.

Latonja peeped through the curtains she had hanging at the window to the right of the door.

Terrance looked down at his feet checking to see if his pants were straight.

Latonja, still standing at the window watching Terrance as he checked himself out, didn't answer the doorbell.

"Mama, what you looking at?"

"Nothing! Go sit down somewhere, boy! You too nosey!" Looking down at her three-year-old son, she motioned for him to leave the room.

"Who is it?" she asked.

"It's me, Terrance."

"I'm coming, give me a minute."

"Come on in, I didn't know you were at the door. How long you been standing here?"

"I've been out here for a while. I was beginning to wonder if the doorbell was broken."

Terrance, slightly annoyed, could only smile.

"Trust me, it ain't broken. These children so loud that it's a wonder I can hear myself think."

"I see you have a lot of unboxing to do. Nice furniture."

Terrance looked around for some place to sit. The blinds and curtains were closed so there was very little lighting in the room.

Latonja laughed.

"Did I say something funny?" Terrance asked.

"Dang, you one uptight brother! Why you act so proper? I told you to chill the other day!"

Latonja threw her hands up in the air as she waited for his reaction.

He stood still waiting on words to come to him.

"I ain't trying to be rude, but you know what I'm saying, right?"

Still waiting on a response from Terrance, she moved clothes from a chair.

Terrance went to sit down but paused for a moment, looked at Latonja and then started dancing.

"No you ain't trying to push it!"

"I still got it. Remember how we used to push it with Salt N Pepa? Stopping to catch a breath, "Is that chilled enough for you?"

"Now, you just plain crazy!"

She laughed out loud and sat down.

"If you need to pinch me, you can do that too."

Terrance extended an arm towards Latonja.

She laughed.

"Sit down crazy boy. Want something to drink?"

Terrance sat down in the chair where Latonja had removed the clothes.

"No thank you. I see you have not changed one bit. You say exactly what's on your mind just like you used to do back in the day.

"That's me. I'm still the same chick from 9th Avenue."

Terrance relaxed his back against the chair.

"You do know your mama brags on you, right?"

"I'm sure she does," replied Terrance.

Terrance rubbed his eyes.

"You sure you don't need some water or something? You look tired."

"I'm good. You ready to leave?"

Terrance stood up.

"Do you know if there is a park close to here?"

"No, but I had planned on going to West Lake."

Terrance sat back down.

"Are you sure you want to go there?"

"Why not?" asked Latonja.

"I can't really say. I just got a bad feeling when you said the name, but if that's where you want to go, then I'm ok with it."

"You tripping Terrance. We used to have fun at that park.

Terrance stood back up.

"I was referring to what happened to Troy there many years ago, but you're right, there were good times there as well."

"Pookie and I didn't go to any other park."

Looking at Terrance, Latonja stood up and proceeded to another room.

"Let me get the boys. We'll be ready in a few minutes."

Thirty minutes later, Latonja had gathered her sons.

Terrance was waiting in the car.

As he drove, Terrance looked in the rearview mirror at Latonja's children in the back seat and then over at Latonja. He wondered why everyone was so quiet.

"I'm sure the park has been updated right?"

Latonja looked forward and took a sip from the soda she was holding.

"They have updated it some."

Approaching the park, Terrance pulled into an empty parking space.

"I would have never imagined that I would have ever returned here," Terrance said with both hands holding the steering wheel.

"Why not?" Latonja asked taking one last sip of her soda.

"To be honest, it reminds me of the day Troy died."

"For real? Like I said, me and Pookie used to come here all the time with the boys. They love it here."

Latonja unbuckled her seat belt and leaned over to the back seat to unbuckle the car seat of her youngest son.

Terrance glanced over at Latonja.

"Ok. Let's get out then so they can play."

"I do know how you feel, but Pookie and I just focused on the good times. The park was not the problem. That fool Lil Man was the problem. They never found out who killed him you know. He was so bad that no one even cared."

Terrance turned the ignition off and unbuckled his seat belt. He sat for a moment to take in the view. At first glance, he didn't see a familiar spot until he looked to his left to see the pool surrounded by a gate. The pool was filled with children. He immediately thought of the day Troy was killed. The pool was a reminder of the last time he saw his friend Troy alive.

Latonja got out and opened the back door of the car on the passenger side. All three of her sons tried to exit at the same time.

"Hold on! Y'all all can't get out at the same time. The park ain't going nowhere, and Terrance what are you doing just sitting there? Are you ok?"

"I'm ok; I guess I had a flashback or something."

Terrance got out of the car and met Latonja on the opposite side of the car.

The boys ran to the swings while Terrance and Latonja sat at a picnic table.

Terrance, with both elbows on the table, leaned in closer to Latonja.

"Were you scared when you got the news about Pookie? Better yet, are you scared now?"

"To be honest, I am scared. I'm scared of being alone. Pookie told me that a picture was going to be missing from my wall. I guess he knew he was going to be gone."

"Don't y'all push each other so hard cause somebody is gonna get hurt!" Latonja yelled at her boys.

She turned her attention back to Terrance.

"Anyway, I know I won't love nobody like I loved him, and I know I won't trust nobody like I trusted him."

"You never know. The right person will come along."

"I don't think so. It's like he is still here with me. I can feel him telling me what to do."

Latonja slightly turned her head away from Terrance to hide the tears in her eyes.

Terrance reached for her hand.

"I have all the confidence in you. I know you and your sons will be fine."

"Terrance, no one outside of my mama and Pookie knew that something bad happened to me when I was a senior in high school. I was raped by my mama's boyfriend. I never liked him living with us. He was always saying things about my body and how I was growing up. I told my mama, but she told me I was being stupid."

"Wait, your mother knew about this and did nothing?"

"Yep, she knew. I guess she just didn't care. You know Mama was always all about herself."

"Yea, I do recall that about her, but that's crazy to think that she knew and did nothing. She could have prevented this from happening to you."

"It's crazy, but he came into my room one day and raped me when nobody else was at home."

Terrance moved his hand away and stood up. "I'm sorry Latonja. I didn't know."

She continued.

"Yea, my mama was something else. The day she found out that I was pregnant, do you know what she did?"

"I can't even guess this one."

"She put me out of her house and nobody but Pookie and me knew why. Pookie knew that I was raped by that monster she called her man. It was a crazy time for Pookie and me both. Pookie let me stay with him."

Pacing in circles around the picnic table, Terrance continued to listen to Latonja talk about what happened to her.

"At the time, Pookie never cared to know if he was the daddy of the baby or not. All he wanted to do was to love me and to protect me."

"I wish you had told someone. It just wasn't right for him or your mother to get away with it."

"It bothered me. I needed to know if that fool was the daddy or if Pookie was the daddy. I had nightmares because I didn't want my baby to have a monster for a daddy."

"I know you say Pookie didn't care, but did you have a paternity test done to determine the father?"

"We finally did on my son's second birthday."

Terrance stopped walking and sat back down at the table.

"Thanks to God the test showed Pookie as the daddy without doubt."

"Whew! You scared me for a minute. I thought you were going to say otherwise."

Latonja looked up and smiled as if she was re-living the moment she found out that Pookie was the father of her son.

"We had the biggest celebration. You know the kind we used to have back in the day. The best part of it all was that nobody but me and Pookie knew what we were celebrating."

Latonja stood up and started walking towards her boys. She expected Terrance to follow as he did. She continued walking and talking with her arms folded.

"Just thinking about it makes me happy. It was a good day for us. Our love was so strong. Pookie protected me."

They had reached the boys on the swings by the time Latonja finished talking about Pookie.

Latonja unfolded her arms and started pushing her son. Terrance held on to one of the poles.

"Sounds like you guys had a special love. I hope everything works out for you. I mean, I know everything will work out for you."

"Thanks for everything. I do appreciate your help. Maybe one day my boys will grow up to be smart like you without being so uptight."

Looking over at Terrance, Latonja smiled.

"They will. I know they will with a mother like you. You don't play girl! And I'm not uptight."

Terrance broke into the same dance as he had at the house.

Latonja reached her arms towards Terrance trying to get him to stop dancing. They both laughed and turned to walk back towards the picnic table.

"Hey, I meant to ask you earlier if you've heard from Charlene?" asked Terrance.

"Somebody said she had moved up North. Don't get me to lying. I don't know who told me that, but I have not heard from her. You know we stopped being friends when she moved from the projects. We had two different circumstances going on."

"You're funny, but you're right. Charlene and her mother were on a mission to get out of the projects."

"What's going on with you. Your mama says you about to get married."

"Yes, it's true. I am very soon," Terrance smiled.

"I want to know everything about her. Like, where she from and is she cute and how did you meet her?"

"Let's see, she is cute. I met her at work, and she's from Mumbai." Holding three fingers up and pushing them down one by one as he answered each question.

"Mumbai, where in the world is that?" asked Latonja stretching her eyes as wide as possible.

"Mumbai is in another country. It's in India."

Terrance chuckled as he watched Latonja's facial expression.

"You mean you marrying a woman from India? Does she wear all of them clothes?"

Terrance, barely, able to speak from laughing looked up.

"Are you done with the questions, or should I go on?" Terrance asked jokingly.

"Yes, go on. I have to hear this."

"She dresses like any other American woman. We love each other very much. You would like her. She's real cool. I'm a lucky man is all I can say."

"That's good to hear."

"She's supportive of my career, and she's all of the other things that a man looks for in a woman. We started out as friends, but I knew from the moment that I met her that she was going to be my wife. She felt the same for me according to her, but we both had to keep our cool since we worked together."

"Sounds like love to me. Just like what I had with Pookie."

"Yes, I'm lucky."

"I still want to meet her to see for myself if she's all right."

"It wouldn't be like you, Latonja, if you didn't."

Terrance smiled and looked over at the car.

"I know you have to go, Terrance, so we better get back, so you can have some time with your mama before you leave."

Latonja stood up and looked over at her children.

Boys! Y'all come on. We have to go so Mr. Terrance can get back to his life in New York," Latonja shouted.

"Thank you, Terrance, for everything. I was only joking about your girlfriend. I don't care where she's from as long as she's good to you. I just want you to be happy because you a good a man. I know I won't be able to make it to the wedding but send me some of the pictures."

"You bet, and she'll be down before the wedding, so you'll have an opportunity to meet her."

Latonja reached for the car door as she gathered her three boys.

"Terrance, I almost forgot to ask but how is your friend Jaylan? Is he still fine?"

Terrance stopped as he reached for the car door.

"Jaylan is cool and married. We still hangout. As a matter of fact, he's the best man in my wedding. He's still Jaylan is all I can say."

"You knew he was crushing on me, right?"

"I'm sure, Latonja."

Terrance pulled up to the house. He opened the car door and stood up with one foot rested on the inside of the door. He watched Latonja get out and gather the boys.

"Take care and remember to be good to yourself. You're a cool person and take care of those boys."

"I will Terrance. I promise you that I will."

The boys all waved goodbye to Terrance and continued to the back yard. Latonja stood and watched Terrance as he drove away.

CHAPTER 2

Reflections

Terrance sat on the plane reflecting on the day he met Priyanka. Being around Latonja and listening to her talk about the love she shared with Pookie made him miss being around Priyanka even more. Terrance reflected on the day he decided to leave the company where he had been employed for nearly four years. Had he not, he would have never met Priyanka.

I knew I had to leave that company. I had been working there for nearly four years with no apparent opportunity to move up in the company. I didn't appreciate it when people I had trained were promoted over me. Patiently, I waited to be promoted, but all I got were false promises and excuses. The final straw was when I was overlooked the third time for a promotion. That promotion was given to an absolute slacker who made so many mistakes that I had to correct for the firm to keep the client's business. That was an eye opener for me. There was no way I was going to sit and let this happen to me again. I talked to my boss about it. I wanted him to look me in my eyes and justify how this guy was promoted over me. I asked him directly, what was the deciding factor? "Terrance, you need to get out more and mingle," he said to me while sitting back in his chair like he was in control of my future career. He went on to give me compliments after I didn't chuckle at his comment as I normally would do. My demeanor said it all. I was not happy, and this was not the time for silly small talk. While he continued to talk, I was planning my next move and questioning why this was happening to me. Would the situation be different if I played golf? No one had ever asked me to join them? I heard the other attorneys talk all the time about it, but they never asked me if I was interested. They acted as if I was not in the room. I had a gut feeling that it was because I was the only black attorney, and they just didn't know how to relate to me. I didn't see it as an excuse to be ignored. I guess I could have asked to be invited to play golf with them, but it didn't seem appropriate. I often wondered why I was the only black attorney, but I tried not to read much into it. The fact of the matter is their lack of diversity was the root of their issues with me, and I could not stay around any longer to allow them to abuse my talent and to give me false hope for a better position. I was not about to spend any more time validating my worthiness.

To say that I was ecstatic to receive an offer from another firm would be an understatement. Two seconds after the call, I typed up my resignation, "It is with mixed emotions," is how I started out the first paragraph. It was the politically correct thing to do because in all honestly, I was glad to get away from that place. I thought about e-mailing it but decided to print a copy to deliver in person. My boss was sitting at his desk when I arrived, and as soon as I walked in the door he resumed his normal position to communicate indirectly that he was in control. I handed him the letter and sat in one of his oversized plush office chairs. I could tell when he completed the first sentence because he paused for a moment and looked at me from the top of his eye glasses. He then cleared his throat and proceeded to read.

He said while looking at me, "Terrance, you are making a mistake. We have a lot of good things in store for you."

I paused before I responded. I needed to think before speaking to be sure my response was delivered unambiguously, and I didn't want to burn any bridges. He was an influential man and well respected in the industry. More so, I didn't hold any grudges. I was not leaving to get back at anyone. My decision to leave was all about me and my career. It was time for me to move on.

Looking him straight in his eyes, I replied, "Thank you and I appreciate the opportunities that I've had here. This, however, is an opportunity that I can't pass up."

He looked away momentarily still holding the letter in his hand. "Well, if there's nothing that I can do to change your mind, good luck to you."

I stood up as that was my cue to leave. I put my hand out for a handshake, but he looked away as if he was angry at my decision. His rudeness didn't burst my bubble. I was going to a new place with better opportunities.

Thirty minutes later after returning to my office, I received a call from the Human Resource Manager. I was asked to come to his office. Once I made it to his office, there he was with my boss and my boss's boss.

My mind wondered what was left to discuss after I had given my resignation. Why was I called to the office like a high school student in trouble? It was strange.

The Director of Human Resources was sitting behind his desk in a chair with a back extending past the top of his head. My boss was sitting in the chair facing to the left of him and his boss was to the right. There was a chair in the far corner of the room positioned where all three men were in direct view. The chair was for me, and it felt to me as if the chair was strategically positioned to intimidate me.

I greeted them all. As I went to sit down, I dropped my pen. I'm sure from my shaking hands. I stooped down to pick up the pen, and that's when I noticed the feet of the Director of Human Resources. His feet were not touching the floor. They were almost dangling. He had them extended with his left foot on top of his right foot and gradually swinging them. Seeing that made me chuckle on the inside. It was all I needed to calm my shaking hands.

"Terrance, we called you in here to give you another chance to change your mind." Those were the words coming from my boss's boss, Mr. Ingle, the same man who barely acknowledged me whenever we passed each other in the hallway.

I looked down at his feet and saw they both were touching the floor, and with both arms resting on each of the arm rest of the chair, I replied, "Well, Mr. Ingle, with all due respect, I don't need another chance. I appreciate the offer, but I've accepted another position with another firm. As I said to Mr. Stiles earlier today when we met, I appreciate the opportunities that I've had here, and I wish the firm continued success."

Mr. Mann, Director of Human Resources, quickly stepped in to add his two cents. "What if we gave you a salary increase and a promotion in six months? I could prepare the documents and have them ready before you leave the room."

My thoughts were screaming, "What are these fools talking about? and "What is the problem with me leaving? What are they worried about?" Is it true what the others whisper? Was I there just to meet some quota? His offer didn't move me or matter to me because I knew it was a false promise, and I had to get away from these strange people. I had moved on the minute I was offered the other job.

"Again, thank you all for the offer, but I've made my decision with great deliberation."

I stood up at that point and shook both of my pants legs one by one to ease the wrinkles from sitting. The other men in the room just sat there. It was awkward, but I walked towards the door. Just as I placed my hand on the doorknob to open the door, I was interrupted by the call of my name.

"Terrance." called Mr. Mann.

I turned momentarily looking back at him.

"We don't need you to give us a two-week notice. Your resignation is effective as you leave this office."

Now, at that point, I almost lost it, but as they had maintained their cool I did the same.

"Thank you, gentlemen, and when can I expect to receive my last paycheck which should include my unused vacation? Oh, and while you are at it, please draw up the necessary documents for my 401k plan. I will need to roll that over to the plan of my new firm. Good day, gentlemen."

They all sat there staring at me as if they had expected a different reaction. It didn't matter to me what they expected. I behaved just as my mother had taught me. I was calm and polite but direct and confident. I closed the door and proceeded to my office to pack up my belongings.

My colleagues stared at me as I was leaving as if they knew I had been asked to leave immediately. No one said a word to me, but I didn't expect them to because it was an awkward moment. My focus was really on bigger and better things.

As I drove away from the building, I thought of the day of my interview at the new firm, the day that I met Priyanka."

The Interview

Terrance entered the office and was greeted by a strikingly beautiful woman at the front desk. He was so taken by her beauty and her smile that he almost forgot why he was there. He hesitated at the sound of her voice.

'May I help you sir?"

Terrance managed to speak to say that he was there for an interview.

She looked down at her calendar and back up at Terrance standing 6'2" tall.

"Are you Terrance Johnson?" she asked.

Nodding yes to answer her question, Terrance looked away.

Noticing that Terrance was struck by her beauty, she extended her hand for a handshake.

"Please have a seat. Mr. Hinkle will be with you shortly."

She, too, was secretly admiring Terrance. Terrance managed to ask her a few questions about the company as he waited.

"Mr. Hinkle will see you now. His office is the third door on the left."

She stood up to point him in the right direction. She extended her hand again for a handshake to wish him luck. Terrance shook her hand but noticed she held on a little longer than the first handshake.

While pulling away to leave for his interview, Terrance smiled looking into her eyes.

Terrance expected to see her again as he was leaving the interview, but she had gone to lunch. He remembered that she had an unusual name but could not remember it.

He decided to look for a business card on her desk. While searching for her business card, he didn't notice that he was being watched by an older woman, with her arms crossed and dressed in a gray pants suit, standing in the corner. He reached for one of the business cards he spotted on the edge of the desk in a card holder.

"May I help you?" the woman asked while uncrossing her arms and walking towards Terrance.

Startled, Terrance quickly moved his hand back without picking up a card.

"Actually, I was looking for a business card of the young lady who was here earlier. I want to send her a thank you note."

"No need for that. I'll give her your message."

Terrance smiled at the woman.

"Thank you and enjoy the rest of your day."

"I will and good luck to you," the woman replied.

Terrance left the office without the business card and regretting that the older woman caught him as he searched for a business card.

Terrance called Jaylan after his interview to see if he was available for lunch. Jaylan was available and agreed to meet him for a late lunch. They planned to meet in Morningside, not very far from where they attended college.

"How did the interview go?" asked Jaylan.

"Great, I think. I got a good vibe from everyone, so I would be surprised if I did not get the job."

"Cool, but you sounded unsure over the phone."

"Nah, that wasn't it. I'm confident the interview went well. I just did something stupid and uncharacteristic of me. I'm just kicking myself."

"Kicking yourself for what?"

"Like I said, I did something stupid. There was this receptionist slash administrative assistant. Hell, I don't know what her position was, but I can't get her out of my head. Man, this woman is beyond beautiful. And the chemistry between us, all I can say is that it was real. I've never experienced anything like it at first sight."

"Get to the point Terrance. Get to the point. What did you do that was stupid?"

"First, I didn't ask her for her number. That was negligence at best on my behalf. It never occurred to me that she would not be there at her desk after my interview."

"Wait, Wait. Tell me, I'm not sitting here listening to you talk about asking a woman for her number while you are on an interview? First, you don't have the job yet, right? And you do want the job, right?" Terrance nodded yes as he listened to Jaylan's point of view. "Then, you did right by not asking her for her number because what if she had reported that? You would have destroyed any possibility of even remotely being considered for the job. Now, if you don't want the job, then that's a different story. I think you want the damn job. Am I Right?"

Terrance interjected, "Of course I do."

Jaylan looked down at the menu.

"Man, you have always been a sucker for good looks. I keep telling you that attitude is going to get you in trouble one day."

"I agree. You're right. Let me stop. It is good that I didn't ask her for her number. There will be plenty of time for that when I get the job."

Jaylan shook his head and laughed. "Man, you're hopeless when it comes to beautiful women."

"I see you married a beautiful woman, so why can't I."

"First, you know nothing about this woman. You don't even know if she has a man or not."

"True, I don't know, but I do know there was mad chemistry there. I refuse to settle for anything less, so don't expect me to settle."

"I'm not asking you to settle, nor do I expect you to settle. I'm just saying look deeper; what's inside counts more than anything else. Melody is a beautiful woman, and I don't mean just her physical attributes. I'm lucky to have found her. She's the complete package. You have a hard time seeing beyond the physical attributes, and that's what worries me about you."

"I hear you. I'm cool. We'll see what happens when I get the job. And you're right. I can't imagine she does not already have a man, but she seemed interested."

Four weeks later, Terrance was called and offered the job. Terrance accepted the offer as a Legal Executive and agreed to start in two weeks. For the first time in his career, Terrance felt valued. The firm's offer was more than he had expected from a responsibility perspective and from a salary perspective.

The minute Terrance accepted the job, he felt an urge to call the woman he had met during his interview but decided to wait until he started his new position. He typed his letter of resignation instead.

FIRST DAY

Driving nearly ten miles above the speed limit on the highway listening to Tupac's "Keep Ya Head Up," Terrance rocked to the beat, momentarily taking his hands off the steering wheel. The lyrics took him from his humble beginnings to where he was at that moment. He then quickly thought of his mother and how supportive she had been through the years. He wanted nothing more than to make her proud. As he exited the highway and waited on the traffic light to change, he looked over at the car to the right of him in the turning lane and saw that a woman was staring at him. She motioned for him to roll down his window.

Terrance turned down his music and rolled down the window.

"I see you are off to a good start this morning," the woman yelled from her car.

Terrance smiled, "I'm starting a new job today!" he yelled back.

"Congratulations. You're looking good this morning. Why don't you pull over, so I can give you my number? We can celebrate later over drinks," the woman replied. Momentarily looking forward, Terrance noticed the traffic light had changed green. He motioned for the beautiful redhead to look forward. "I would love to, but I can't be late on my first day. Fate has it, maybe we'll meet again on this path." The woman smiled and made her right turn and looked in her rearview mirror to see that Terrance had made his left turn and was heading to his new job with his music turned up continuing to rock to Tupac's "Keep Ya Head Up".

Stepping out of his car, Terrance looked down at his shoes to be sure that his pants were straight and not tucked into the back of his shoe. He wiped his hands across his face and blew into his cuffed hands to check his breath. He wanted to make a good impression his first day on the job.

He walked up to the building, stopped and looked up as far as he could to see to the top of the building. The building was 50 floors high. He wanted to pinch himself, but he smiled instead and proceeded to enter the building. He said "hello" to just about everyone he passed. Many people took a second look as he passed.

Finally, making it to his office on the 30th floor, he pulled the door open towards him. He was expecting to see the woman he had been thinking about since first meeting her. Disappointed that the chair was empty, he paused for a moment and then proceeded to the area where people gathered for coffee and morning conversation.

"Hello everyone, I don't mean to interrupt your conversations, but I'm new here and wanted to take a moment to introduce myself."

"Welcome," one lady stated as she moved towards him to shake his hand.

Everyone else followed her. He was greeted with many smiles and introductions. Although there were too many names and faces for him to remember, he was happy to receive a warm welcome from everyone he met.

Terrance did notice a familiar face. The face of the older woman he also met the day of his interview. He remembered her watching him as he searched the desk for a business card. She not only introduced herself as Harriet but also as his assistant.

Harriet gave him a tour around the office and eventually to an office that was connected to her space. Her space was located right outside of Terrance's office. There was no getting to Terrance's office without passing her desk.

The girl of his dreams still nowhere in sight, Terrance hoped that she was just late coming to the office. He wanted to ask Harriet about her but worried she would remember he had inquired about her right after his interview.

There were other females in the office more than willing to show Terrance around to get to know him. He could feel many of them glaring at him, but he wanted nothing more than to see the girl he had met during his interview.

Eager to know, he couldn't wait any longer. He didn't care if Harriet remembered him as the guy trying to steal a business card off the desk.

"Where's the girl who sits at the front desk?"

"You mean Priyanka?" she asked.

"I don't recall her name."

"Then describe her. Anyone could have been sitting at the front desk." Harriet knew very well who Terrance was referring to.

Pausing before he attempted to describe her, he thought of what Harriet might think if he described her as beautiful.

"I can't really say, but I don't think she's from here. Maybe from India?"

"Then you are asking about Priyanka."

"Does she still work here? I haven't seen her yet, so I was just wondering."

"Terrance, has she been on your mind since you first met her? It seems that way to me. Listen, I don't mean to get into your business, but Priyanka should not be your priority. And to be honest with you, all I know is that she is on vacation. I don't know where she is or when she will be back."

"No, I really didn't come here looking for her. I don't want you to get the wrong impression. I spoke to her on the day of my interview. I just wanted to say hello."

"I remember. You were curious then, searching the desk for a business card, and you're curious now. I was not born yesterday, Terrance. All I'm saying is that your focus should be on your accounts. You have some big accounts, and you don't want to screw up anything. The higher-ups are depending on you to turn things around."

Taken by her tone, Terrance looked away embarrassed that he had allowed himself to ask about the girl he could not get off his mind.

"You are so right, and I appreciate your concern. I think we are going to make a great team."

Harriet smiled and walked over to Terrance. Patting him on the shoulder she whispered, "You're not the first to be taken by her beauty, but office romances are never a good thing."

Smiling at Harriet as he turned to go to his office, he hit himself on his head.

"Thanks again for your advice. Can you pull the files of the accounts that are most important and need immediate attention?"

Harriet walked over to the file cabinet to pull the files with a smile on her face.

A week later, Priyanka returned to work. Terrance didn't ask about her anymore after his conversation with Harriet. Instead he stayed focused and worked closely with Harriet to learn more about the issues with his accounts.

Priyanka developed her strategy to win Terrance's heart over the other single women in the office as soon as she heard that Terrance had accepted the job. She knew based on the buzz amongst the single women in the office that she would have competition for Terrance's attention. She decided to take a few days off during Terrance's first week to give the other women in the office a chance to throw themselves at him all at once. She wanted all the attention to herself. She remembered the attraction she and Terrance felt towards each other when they first met, but she didn't know if he remembered. She studied his employee file to learn more about him; the fact that he was highly educated and unmarried made her want him even more. She didn't know if he was single nor did she care. All that mattered to her was that he was not married. Although she was absent for the first week of his employment, she was not worried about competing with the other women. She knew how to win over the competition when it came to men.

Priyanka told everyone she was going away for her vacation. She actually stayed home to get plenty of rest, so she could look extra special for Terrance. She bought several new outfits but a special one for the first day of her return to the office. There was no doubt in her mind that Terrance was attracted to her. She knew being away would only create more desire for her.

Standing at the door of the office in a form-fitting multi colored dress cut just above her knees with high-heeled shoes, Priyanka said, "Excuse me."

"Yes?" replied Terrance without looking up from the file he was working on to see who was standing at the door.

Terrance then looked up when no one replied. He felt as if his heart had stopped when he saw that it was Priyanka.

"Hey you, come on in."

Terrance stood up as she entered the room.

Harriet also looked up. "Oh my God, I knew this day was coming," she whispered to herself as Priyanka entered the office.

"I just wanted to peep in to welcome you."

She extended her hand for a handshake. "I'm Priyanka. It's so good to see you again. I knew you were going to get the job."

"And how did you know that?"

Giggling in a girlish manner, curling a few strands of her hair with her finger, she replied, "Let's just say I added my two cents."

"Anyway, I won't take up any more of your time. I just stopped by to welcome you. Let me know if you need anything. I run things around here."

"Really?"

"No, I'm joking with you. But do let me know if you need anything."

"Wait, let me introduce myself. I'm Terrance. Terrance Johnson that is, and I'm happy to meet you."

Standing with crossed legs at this point, Priyanka smiled. "I see you got jokes. I like that. But I completed all your paperwork, so I know a little more about you than your name."

Terrance could tell from Priyanka's comment and the way she was flirting that she was just as interested in him as he was in her.

Priyanka looked over at Harriet and saw Harriet was annoyed.

"I'll let you get back to work. Please don't forget to let me know if you need anything."

Harriet had heard enough and decided to end the mutual flirting.

"We do have a lot of work to do, Priyanka, but thanks for stopping by. I'm sure Terrance will let you know if he needs anything."

"Sure, Harriet, I didn't mean to stop anyone from working. I just wanted to peep in to welcome Terrance and to let him know that I'm here if he needs me for anything."

Terrance looked over at Harriet's expression and then back over to Priyanka. He knew enough about women to know that a silent catfight was in motion, so he decided to intervene.

"No problem, Priyanka. I appreciate you stopping by and I'll come by your desk later because there are some supplies that I do need to order."

PRIYANKA

Thinking back to when he first met Priyanka stirred up unpleasant memories as well. Priyanka was not happy about Terrence leaving for Alabama. He thought of her attitude the morning of his flight. She wanted nothing more than for him to move forward in life without looking back to the past or the people from his past. There were times he felt she didn't want him talking about his own family. She didn't like hearing about the hard times Terrance experienced while growing up.

"Terrance, you have to learn to accept that some people choose to stay where they are in life and will never do any better."

Terrance would try to reason with her to get her to see that not all people are in situations by choice. No matter the length or intensity of the conversation, Priyanka held on to her strong opinion.

She took pride in the fact that she and Terrance were both college educated. She feared that once she and Terrance had their own family, he would share his past with their children, and she would not want their children to know that such a life existed.

As much as Terrance didn't like this side of Priyanka, it was her beauty, kindness, and intellect that attracted him the most. He was sure that one day she would see things as he did and would change her opinion.

The Beginning

Each day at the office, Priyanka would insert herself into Terrance's day, asking him questions about clients as she mailed paperwork at Harriet's request or anything else she could think of. She assumed he knew where she was born because everyone in the office did, but she was curious why he had never asked her about it. One day while Terrance was having lunch in the company's break room, she decided to go up to him to inquire.

"Hi Terrance. How are you?"

"I'm good and, how are you?"

"I'm great but just curious about something," replied Priyanka while standing and forcing Terrance to look up at her.

"What's that?"

"Do you know where I was born?"

"I assumed somewhere in India. Am I correct?"

"Yes, Mumbai. I guess that's not of interest to you?"

"No, that's not it at all. I think it's cool. I enjoy meeting people from other places. I have just been so busy that I have not had the chance to get to know anyone on a personal level."

Pulling a chair out, Priyanka sat, leaned forward and whispered, "Well, maybe you and I will have that chance one day."

Pausing before responding, Terrance looked around the room to see if anyone was watching. Turning back to face Priyanka, "Maybe," he replied.

Priyanka then smiled, stood up and walked away slowly. She looked back expecting to catch Terrance watching as she walked away, but instead Terrance was back to eating and looking over some documents.

Harriet happened to be in the break room having lunch with friends. She sat back and watched as Priyanka and Terrance talked. It was obvious to her and everyone else in the office that Priyanka was after Terrance. She knew that Priyanka eventually would find a way to have time with him alone. Terrance was intrigued by her beauty but had become more involved in his work and had not pursued a relationship with Priyanka as he thought he would. Priyanka could see that other women in the office were finding reasons to talk to him as well. And because Terrance had not asked her out she didn't know if he was interested in her anymore. One day, while on his way to his car, Priyanka decided that she was going to invite him to her place for dinner.

"Terrance!" she called as he was opening his car door. "You should come over for dinner tonight. I'm making my favorite Indian dish. I would love for you to come over to taste it. You won't regret it."

Standing still with his key in his hand and looking towards her with curious eyes.

"I would love to, but are you sure that it's not against some company policy?"

"I won't tell if you don't," she replied.

Looking down at the key in his hand, he pressed the button to unlock the car door.

"Sure, you can give me the directions to your place when I get back to the office."

Priyanka smiled and walked away. Terrance looked at her as she disappeared into the building before driving away.

"Sir, would you like anything to drink or a small snack?" The flight attendant asked.

Terrance was not asleep but was in deep thought, still thinking back about Priyanka.

"Coke and peanuts would be fine."

Drifting back to when Priyanka invited him over for dinner, Terrance knew after that dinner date that Priyanka was the girl he was going to introduce to his mother and the woman that he would marry. He enjoyed every moment he spent talking that night. He was intrigued when listening to her talk about her culture, and the food spoke to his heart.

The next day in the office it was clear to Priyanka that Terrance was into her. She felt she had to let the other girls in the office know so they would stop flirting with him. She rarely joined the others in the break room; however, the day after having dinner with Terrance, she joined three women in the break room who she felt were interested in Terrance. She wanted them to know all about her date with Terrance the night before. They were shocked when she walked over and pulled up a chair to sit at the table with them.

"You ladies don't care if I join you, do you?"

"No, not at all," one woman replied.

"Girl, what's been up with you lately? You are always so busy. I'm surprised you're even taking time for lunch today," said another.

"Yea, what's up with you girl?" asked the third woman.

They knew that Priyanka had a reason for wanting to join them.

"Well, if you ladies must know. I invited Terrance over to my house last night."

"Great, Terrance is a cool guy," replied one woman.

"I'm sorry, where are my manners? Are any of you interested in him?"

They all looked at each other momentarily before the same woman spoke.

"Girl, each of us have our own men. Terrance is cool and all, but there's no interest among us. Right ladies?"

"Right and we wish you all the best, but if I were you, I would keep it quiet around the office," replied another one of the women.

"I will and thanks for your advice. We had such a good time talking, and he loved the food I cooked. He couldn't stop talking about it. I know I shouldn't say this, but I trust you ladies. He pulled me close to him and kissed me before I knew it. I tried to resist, but to be honest, I couldn't. In my 29 years of life, I have never been kissed like Terrance kissed me. It was so tender, and he's so masculine. He was the perfect gentleman. He is a perfect man in every way is all I can say."

The woman looked at each other as if they were sick to their stomachs.

"Girl, it was good catching up with you, but we better get back to work."

All three ladies stood up and left Priyanka sitting at the table alone.

"I'll see you ladies around. Thanks for letting me join you," Priyanka stated as the ladies walked away.

Priyanka's beauty could be quite intimidating, but her smile and demeanor made her very approachable and liked. There were, however, women in the office, including Harriet, who felt that Priyanka was hiding something behind that smile and was not always truthful. She could carry on a conversation without giving anyone an opportunity to ask any questions. People knew only what Priyanka wanted them to know about her. She was full of stories about her culture. She made it known that she was raised in New York, which was her explanation for why she did not have an Indian accent. She was proud to say that she was born in Mumbai. She told the same story of how her parents moved to New York when she was only a few months old and that she would often travel back to Mumbai to visit her other relatives up until she was twelve years old.

Priyanka would get sad when she told the story of how her parents became embarrassed about her at age twelve and refused to take her back to visit her relatives in Mumbai. They felt she had adapted to American culture. Tears would come to her eyes when she described how her parents asked her to leave their home when she was only eighteen years old. She would end the story by saying that she loved and missed her family but was proud of herself for making it on her own.

When asked if she ever tried to contact her family to make peace, she would say that her culture was very strict and that it was not possible for her to ever see her parents again. She explained that she had accepted the fact that her family would never be a part of her life.

Often, Priyanka would come to social events dressed in her culture clothing. When asked if there was a special reason she was wearing the clothing, she would answer that she was missing her mother and father.

Priyanka was slim and stood five feet six inches tall with slight curves and captured attention everywhere she went. She had shoulder length, black, straight, silky hair. Her teeth were as white as pearls, and her skin was flawless and the color of lightly cooked caramel.

Polite and intelligent, Priyanka was full of conversation whether the subject was politics or entertainment.

It was Priyanka's confidence, smile and beauty that captured Terrance. He had never met a woman with such beauty and confidence.

"Ladies and gentlemen thank you for flying Delta. We will be landing in about three minutes in LaGuardia Airport."

CHAPTER 3

Natalie

N o matter how much they worked or gave to their four children, it was never enough for their oldest child Natalie.

Natalie's father worked for a local distribution company driving a forklift, and her mother worked as a sales associate at Sears.

Natalie's parents struggled financially at times, but they provided well for their children. They lived in a middle-class neighborhood where the school system was one of the top in the state of Wisconsin. Natalie wanted more. She wanted her parents to have college degrees and professional jobs as did the parents of most of her friends.

Natalie was polite to most of her peers at school, but her closest friends were the wealthiest at the school or were athletes. She felt they were the most ambitious and that she could learn how to become wealthy if she surrounded herself with them.

Because of the struggles of her parents, Natalie had adopted a motto that she was not living the same way twice. She was never appreciative of the clothes her mother bought for her even when she was complimented by her friends.

"This outfit is from Sears, purchased with my mother's discount. No need for a compliment," Natalie would respond.

Although her friends thought she was unappreciative and unfair to her parents, they never expressed that to her because they feared she would stop talking to them and would get others to do the same. Each day they would listen to Natalie talk about what her parents didn't have.

Natalie was a bright student with mediocre grades, doing what she had to do to just get by. She was told by each of her teachers that she had the potential to be an "A" student. Natalie didn't care and had about as much respect for her teachers as she had for her parents.

Although Natalie was one of the most popular girls in school, she felt she didn't receive the respect she desired because her parents were not wealthy. She wanted wealth to go with her beauty, and she grew angrier each day at her parents for not providing her with the material things her friends had.

Natalie's boyfriend, Mark, was on the football team. He was a starting player but not the quarterback. She wanted the quarterback Grant, but he had a girlfriend. Mark didn't know that Natalie was first interested in Grant. She wanted Grant for more reasons than one. He was not only a great athlete but also the only son of one of the wealthiest men in the state. Grant's family was well liked and respected in the community not only because of their wealth but because they were kind people willing to help the less fortunate. Grant's girlfriend, Meredith, also came from a wealthy well-connected family, and she was just as beautiful as Natalie.

Natalie felt that Grant would have chosen her over Meredith had she come from a wealthy family. She felt that she was more attractive than Meredith, but people could not see it because of who her parents were.

Natalie's parents noticed an increase in her irritability. They tried talking to her to see if she would talk to them about what was making her so angry, but Natalie didn't talk. She only yelled at her parents and would slam the door to her bedroom whenever they tried to talk to her.

Natalie's parents thought Natalie's behavior was typical of a teenager. They tried not to get into any confrontations with Natalie to avoid upsetting their younger children.

Natalie spent a lot of time over to her boyfriend's house. Mark's parents were not on the same financial level as Grant's parents, but they were professionals. For that reason, Natalie had more respect for Mark's parents than she had for her own parents.

One day while visiting Mark, Natalie stood on the porch watching Mark and his father work in the yard. "Now there's a man that has done well for his family. What were my parents thinking when they had children?" she thought.

Looking around, she compared her house to Mark's. Natalie lived in a modest ranch house built in the 70's. Her parents kept the house neat and clean and the yard well groomed. Mark lived in a two-story modern brick house built in the 80's. As she watched Mark and his father, she continued to compare her father to Mark's father. When Mark's father pulled his lawn mower from the garage, she thought of how her father would sometimes borrow the neighbor's lawn mower when theirs went out. "Why can't he just buy a new lawn mower?" she said out loud before realizing it. Mark and his father looked over at her, but she quickly looked away.

Natalie often had dinner with Mark and his parents. They enjoyed talking with Natalie. Mark had asked Natalie on several occasions if she would bring her parents over to meet his parents. Natalie told him that her parents would not be interested because they were not happy with her relationship with him. One day while helping Mark's mother clean up after dinner, Mark's mother decided to have a conversation with Natalie about her relationship with Mark.

"Natalie, Mark tells me that your parents are not happy about your relationship with Mark. Is it Mark that they do not like, or is it something else?"

"Oh no, it's not Mark at all. I didn't want to say anything because I didn't think you all would understand. I didn't want you all to have a negative view of me, but my parents do not like anyone to be honest. All they do is criticize me. I cannot do anything right in their eyes. They call me stupid and anything else they can think of. I know you have invited them over several times, but I never told them because they will only get mad at me."

"Oh my, I'm sorry to hear. But are you ok? They don't hit you, do they?"

"No, they don't. They just don't talk to me and they look at me like I'm nothing. I like coming over here because you guys have so much love in your family. It's my way of escaping what I must deal with at home. I hope you don't mind."

"No, we don't mind at all. You are a beautiful, special girl who is going places in life. You are welcomed over here any time you like."

"Thank you. I better get home now before they get mad at me for coming home late."

As time progressed towards the end of senior year, Natalie spent more and more time with Mark although her desire for Grant grew stronger with each passing day. She wanted nothing more than to prove to Meredith that she could have Grant.

Each day after school Grant waited around for Meredith. Meredith had swim practice that ran thirty minutes later than football practice. Secretly watching Grant from a distance, Natalie planned how she was going to make her move on him.

Seeing Meredith walk towards Grant with her perfect legs and swinging her long blonde hair caused Natalie to hate her even more.

Thirty minutes was all she had to get Grant's attention as he waited for Meredith.

One day, feeling that it was time, she walked up to Grant and started a conversation.

"Hey, I see you here every day."

She sat down on the bench next to him leaving only a small space between them.

"Yeah, I am here every day waiting for my girlfriend to get out of swim practice."

"Cool, then you don't mind me keeping you company until she's out."

"No, but why are you here? Waiting on someone? You're Mark's girl, right?"

"Yes, Mark and I are seeing each other. I wait around here for my father to pick me up."

"Mark can't give you a ride home?"

"He can, but my father won't allow it. It's not a problem. It actually gives me time to catch up on some homework."

"I guess you are all caught up today?"

"Not really, I just thought I would come over to say hello. You don't mind, do you? Or will you get in trouble with Meredith?"

"Nah, Meredith's cool. You do know her, right?"

"Yes. I know her. Who doesn't know her?"

They smiled and continued their conversation.

At first, Grant didn't know what to think of Natalie. It was hard for him to tell if she was coming on to him or if she was just being friendly. It was when they had talked every day for a week that Natalie confessed to him her true feelings for him. Natalie was beautiful. Her charm, her beauty and her smile captivated him, despite his being in love with Meredith. Grant was confused, but he could not resist Natalie the day she enticed him to follow her to an unused closet in the gym. The closet became their secret meeting place for nearly a month.

One day while at his locker, Grant overhead Natalie talking to one of her friends about how he was going to break up with Meredith so that he can openly date her.

Grant didn't appreciate the conversation because he had no intentions of breaking up with Meredith. Later that day he did not show up to meet Natalie. He stayed outside in his car and waited for Meredith. As the days passed, he avoided Natalie in the hallways, and he never showed up again to their secret closet. Natalie eventually got the message. She did not ask Grant why he stopped showing up because she didn't want him to think she cared. She didn't tell Meredith about sneaking around with Grant because she did not want it to get back to Mark.

Ignoring her parent's rules, Natalie came home two to three hours late each day after school. She spent those late hours with Mark and his parents. She never bothered to ask her parents for permission or to let them know that she was going to Mark's house.

Natalie's parents knew she had become rude and disrespectful to them but didn't know she had started to neglect her school work. They received a call from the principal's office late in the semester. Natalie had been hiding grades from them. They were told that Natalie was running the risk of not graduating high school.

Waiting for her to come home from school, Natalie's parents sat in the living room eager to talk to her about what they had learned from speaking with the principal.

"What now?" Natalie asked as she saw both parents sitting in the living room.

No one ever used that room, so Natalie knew something was up.

"Sit down, Natalie." replied Natalie's father.

"Why, what did I do now?"

"Natalie, we are not going to argue with you. Things must change around here. You are spinning out of control. You're disrespectful to us, your teachers and Lord knows what else you have been doing."

"We are worried about you. Something has to change," her mother added after her father spoke.

"This is stupid. Don't talk to me anymore. I'm going to my room."

Natalie motioned to leave the room.

"Sit down Natalie! We are tired of your disrespect!" replied her father.

"Why are you yelling? I came home to bother no one. I don't ask for anything, so why are you yelling at me?"

"Natalie, listen for a minute. The principal of your school called today. You are failing honey. You may not graduate if you don't start doing your work. He is going to give you a chance to make up what you've missed so that you can graduate." Her mother stated.

Natalie sat on the sofa and crossed her arms.

"Your father and I don't understand what is going on with you. Are we supposed to sit back and let you fail? Starting tomorrow, you are not allowed to go to Mark's after school. We are expecting you to be here at home after school."

"Your mother and I are serious, Natalie. We have tried to be understanding, but you are too far out of line."

Natalie stood up.

"I rather just live with Mark and his family."

"Who gave you that option? Your mother and I clearly didn't."

"Dad, you can barely take care of us, so you should be happy. You will have one less person to feed. I eat over to Mark's basically every day anyway."

"Like I said, who gave you that option?"

"Mark's dad is far more of a man than you. Mark's mom does not have to work if she does not want to."

"Who do you think you are talking to? I'm not going to sit back and let you talk to me any way in my house!"

"Calm down! The both of you need to calm down!"

Natalie turned to face her mother.

"Mom, you are just as bad. You walk around here like you have made it, but you are no better. You are weak. I can't take it here anymore. I'm taking my pregnant self to live with Mark and his family!"

Natalie ran from the living room to the kitchen and exited the house through the back door.

Natalie's mother held her husband back to keep him from running after Natalie. She then ran after Natalie and was able to talk Natalie back into the house.

Natalie sat at the kitchen table with her parents to talk.

"I'm sorry Dad. I didn't' mean to say those mean things to you. I really do love you and Mom. Why didn't you and mom go to college so that you could have real careers instead of the stupid jobs you have? It's so damn embarrassing to have uneducated parents, which is why I want to raise this baby with Mark and his family."

"So, being pregnant and cursing at your parents is not embarrassing? This is your mistake Natalie. We did nothing but love you. You can't blame us for your mistake," stated her father.

"Are you calling my baby a mistake?"

"No baby, your father is not calling your baby a mistake, but your actions are leading you down the wrong road. We just had higher hopes for you."

"Are you saying that because I'm pregnant that my future is going to be limited to a sales clerk like you?"

"No, Natalie, I'm not saying that. I'm just saying it's going to be harder than not having a baby, but you have the support of your father and me. We will figure it out so that you can finish high school and go to college here."

"Sounds like you want me to turn out like you. I'm not staying here. You and Dad are lazy and will never be more than what you are. I can't believe how content the two of you are with living the way you do. I'm going to live with Mark and his family. They know how to live the way that I want to live."

Standing up and walking away, Natalie didn't look back at her parents as she headed to her room.

Confused and disappointed, Natalie's parents sat at the dining room table and watched Natalie as she left the room. They decided not to follow her to give her time to think and to get over her anger.

The next morning Natalie's mother went into Natalie's room to check on her but found that she had left the house, apparently during the early morning hours.

Mark's mother called just as Natalie's father was about to leave the house to look for her. Mark's mother explained that Mark had come to pick Natalie up during the early morning hours after receiving a frantic call from Natalie saying that she had no place to go.

"I'm calling just to let you know that Natalie is with us, and she is doing fine. How could you put your teenaged daughter out on the streets?" Kids make mistakes but, how could you?"

Natalie's mother moved the phone away from her ear to let her husband listen in. She could not believe what she was hearing.

"Hang up! We don't have to listen to this, just hang up!" stated Natalie's father.

Natalie's mother put the phone closer to her ear and away from her husband's ear. He walked away and went to the next room.

"Now, may I speak?"

"Sure."

"First, I don't appreciate you calling us with your accusations. There are always two sides to a story. Had the situation been reversed, I would have called you and your husband like a responsible adult to get the other side of the story. So please, don't ever call our house again accusing us of mistreating our daughter. Natalie told us about the baby, too. She didn't give us time to talk to her. She stormed away to her room. We assumed she was in for the night and were going to continue our conversation with her the next morning. We felt she needed time to cool off. As we now know, she left the house. We didn't know. We would never put our daughter out on the streets. I don't know what Natalie told you folks, but you were not told the truth."

Mark's mother listened without interrupting.

"I apologize. I should have called you as soon as she called Mark. My husband, Mark and I took Natalie for her word. She was so upset that she could barely speak. I don't know how you feel about it, but at this point I think it's best to let Natalie stay over here until she's calm. At least you know she's in a safe place. Talk it over with your husband and give us a call back tonight."

"Sure, I'll talk to my husband, but I can tell you now that we are not going to allow her to call the shots."

Hanging up the phone, she turned to see her husband standing close behind her, waiting to hear what was said after he left the room.

"I agreed to allow Natalie to stay over there until she comes to her senses, but as I told Mark's mother, we can't allow Natalie to call the shots. She's still a child."

He sat down at the table and rested his face in the palm of his hands before looking up at his wife.

"I think it's best for us all. Natalie is not a child. She's nearly eighteen years old and will be graduating high school soon. Clearly, she has some issues and at this point we can't force her to do anything. She won't even listen to us. Natalie is going to do what Natalie wants to. We can try to force her, but she'll be out the door as soon as she turns eighteen."

"I don't know where we went wrong."

Natalie's mother looking into the eyes of her husband, sat in the chair next to him and rested her head on his shoulder."

Feeling the trembling body of his wife, he rubbed her back.

"Don't worry. Natalie will be home. She'll come to her senses, and we'll support her and the baby."

"I pray you are right." She replied.

"But we have to prepare ourselves if she decides she is not coming back." stated Natalie's father.

"Why would you say something like that? You act like you don't care if she comes back or not."

"Were you even listening to her last night? She thinks nothing of us. We are lazy good for nothing people in her eyes. It sickens me to think that she could go to Mark's family and just outright lie on us. What is wrong with that girl?"

Standing still for a moment, Natalie's mother looked at her husband and walked away without responding to his question.

He left the room to attend to their other children.

A few weeks passed, and Natalie had not contacted her parents. Mark's mother periodically called to let Natalie's mother know that Natalie was ok and was doing well in school. She was happy to hear that Natalie was doing well in school but saddened that Natalie didn't want to have anything to do with her family. It was that moment that Natalie's mother realized that Natalie was not coming home and that she needed to focus on her other children more. She had become so depressed that her husband was doing all the cooking and taking care of their other children while she worked and slept.

Natalie continued to go to school each day. It was as if she had become a new person. She was excited that she was finally living the life she had dreamed about. She and Mark's mother went shopping almost every day. She and Mark's parents went out to dinner a couple of nights a week. She didn't care that she was pregnant because she knew that Mark's parents were going to take care of both her and the baby, and she could have anything she wanted. She and Mark had talked about attending college in town. It was not until she walked in on a conversation between Mark and his mother that she discovered that Mark had different plans than what he had discussed with her.

"What's going on? Why all the excitement? It can't be the baby because I still have a couple of months?"

Mark and his mother looked at each other not knowing how to respond.

"Mark received a football scholarship to LSU."

"Wait, LSU? What do you mean? Mark is going to school here. He didn't even apply anywhere else."

Mark's mother knew at that moment that Natalie knew nothing of the plans she and her husband had discussed with Mark. Mark stood still trying to figure a safe way out of the conversation.

"Natalie, my parents are going to keep the baby so that we can go to school in Louisiana."

"What do you mean? Mark, you know that I have not applied anywhere! I'm barely graduating so what damn school in Louisiana or anywhere else do you think is going to accept me into their program?"

"You never know. All you have to do is to apply, and I'm sure there are community colleges there."

"So, when were you going to tell me so that I could apply? Never mind, don't hurt yourself trying to answer. I see what's going on here, nothing but lies!"

"Natalie, calm down. I was going to tell you. I wanted to see what was going to happen with me first."

"What's going on is that you and your family have plotted against me. What is going to happen to me? You all think only of this baby and to hell with you all! What if I told you this may not even be your baby? Then what? I would not make any plans for this baby if I were you all!" Natalie exited the room leaving Mark and his mother standing looking at each other.

"Mark, that girl is evil, and I want her out of my house today! Did you hear what she just said? The baby may not even be yours! We have spent so much time and money preparing for a grandchild that may not be ours!"

"Mom, now you need to calm down. Natalie is just being emotional. We should have told her that LSU had expressed an interest in me. Let me handle this mom. She is just upset."

Mark's father entered the house from work to hear the tail end of the conversation between Mark and his mother.

"What's all the yelling? I could hear you all from the door."

Mark explained everything to his father. His father agreed with him and told Mark's mother to allow Mark to handle the situation.

Natalie returned to the room after speaking with Mark. She apologized for her outburst.

"I was upset because I was reminded of how I was treated by my parents. I'm always invisible to people for some reason. It's like I don't matter to anyone. No one asked me about my future. What am I supposed to do? What is going to happen to me and the baby while Mark goes off to school?"

"Natalie, I won't leave you hanging. All my plans include you and the baby. Going to LSU is going to mean big things for us. Do you know how many professional players come out of LSU? This is a big opportunity for us. You, me and the baby will be set for life."

Mark's mother didn't feel that Natalie's apology was sincere, but she went along with it just to keep peace for her son.

It's a Boy

Two months later, Natalie delivered a seven-pound baby boy, twenty-one inches long. Although excited, Mark was reminded by his mother that he needed to get a paternity test done to remove any doubt. Natalie saw Mark's mother whispering to him as she was talking to Mark's father.

"Mark, I've ordered a paternity test. The nurse should be in here shortly."

Mark walked away from his mother to the bedside of Natalie.

"I trust you. You don't have to do this."

"Mark, say no more. I know you trust me. It's not a matter of trust. I spoke out of anger, so it's because of me your mother has her doubts."

With pursed lips, Mark's mother left the room.

Mark's mother had contacted Natalie's parents to let them know that Natalie had delivered a baby boy. She was sure that Natalie had not called her parents.

Eager to see their daughter and grandson, Natalie's parents went to the nursery first to see their grandson. Mark's mother was waiting for Natalie's parents near the nursery. She had never met them face to face before.

Walking up to the man and women standing at the nursery window, she asked if they were Natalie's parents.

"Thank you for calling us. How's Natalie?" asked Natalie's mother.

"Natalie is fine. I'm sorry I have not been in touch with you in person before now, and I'm sorry if I ever made you feel bad in any way."

"Say no more. We are just happy that Natalie and the baby are both doing well."

Standing and smiling as they watched their grandson behind the glass window in the center of all the other new born babies, Natalie parents embraced each other. Looking away from the baby for brief moments, they discussed the different characteristics of their grandson.

"I can already see that he has Natalie's beautiful smile and your big eyes," stated Natalie's father.

"I know, look at those cheeks, and he has Natalie's perfect smooth skin," Natalie's mother replied.

After staring at their grandson for fifteen minutes, Natalie's parents headed to visit with Natalie.

Natalie looked at her parents as they entered the room. She had no visible emotions, so her parents didn't know if they were welcomed. They felt the coldness of her stare.

Walking closer to the bed, Natalie's mother leaned over to give Natalie a kiss on her right cheek as she reached her bedside. She could feel Natalie pull away slightly as if she didn't want to be touched by her. Natalie's father then leaned over to give her a quick peck on the cheek. He could feel that Natalie didn't want them there. He watched how Natalie looked he and his wife up and down as if she disapproved of what they were wearing. He ignored it because through it all he was happy to see that his daughter and grandson were both doing well.

Natalie had very few words for her parents. Her mother tried to make small talk and spoke nothing of Natalie coming back home.

"How's school sweetheart?" her mother asked.

"Fine I guess. I finished all of my classes."

Natalie looked over at Mark standing in the corner.

"When is graduation?"

"I really don't know."

Natalie then turned back to Mark.

"Mark, can you pour me some water?"

She looked at her mother as she reached for the cup of water from Mark.

"I'm not worried about graduation. I've completed the work. I'm going to Community College in the fall."

"That's great honey. I'm so proud of you."

Arms folded, Natalie's father watched as his wife talked to Natalie.

"Mark's mother is going to take care of the baby while I attend classes."

"I'm available to help too, honey. I would like nothing more than to spend time with my grandbaby."

"Thanks, but we have it all worked out. She barely works because she does not have to, so her schedule will be easier to work around my class schedule."

Natalie's father interrupted before his wife could respond.

"Sounds like you have it all worked out. Your mother just wants you to know that she is available if you need her."

Natalie made a grunting noise and placed her hands across her stomach.

"I'm getting tired. Can I ask you and mom to leave now?"

"Sure, sure, we are so excited that we forgot you are probably tired," replied her mother.

"Before we go, have you named him?" asked her father.

"Oh, yes for sure. We named our son Justin. He was named after Mark's uncle. He owns his own business."

Natalie's father placed his hands on his head, looked at Natalie and walked away without saying good bye.

"I love you Natalie, and I'll always be your mother. You know where to reach me if you need me."

With her husband waiting at the doorway, she took his hand as he held it out.

"This hurts more than anything I could have ever imagined. I never thought that I could raise a child to hate me so much. How can I learn to live with a sad heart?"

"Honey, don't beat yourself up over Natalie. You gave her so much. You were there for her as a mother."

"But why does she hate me so much?"

"I don't think she hates you. I think she hates herself for the way she has behaved. One day she will realize it, and hopefully she will find a way to live without regret over the way she has treated us."

"I should have been a better, stronger mother. I ask myself repeatedly where I went wrong, and I still don't know why she despises us so much."

"Stop it now! You have other children to worry about. Natalie has her reasons, and there is nothing we can do but pray and ask God to watch over her. She's his child now. We have done what we could."

Natalie's father stood next to his wife, rubbing her back as she continued to express the hurt she was feeling. He was silently hurting too but felt he had to be strong for his wife. He prayed that God would take the pain away from his wife and help her to deal with the realization that Natalie wanted nothing to do with them. She was not coming home.

Four months after graduation, Mark left for college leaving Natalie and the baby behind with his parents. Natalie registered for paralegal classes at the community college.

Mark was able to visit with Natalie and his son twice before his first game. Natalie spoke to Mark's parents several times, asking them to pay for her and her son to visit Mark, but they disapproved. They wanted Mark to stay focused on school and football. They felt that Natalie would be a distraction. They thought it was bad enough that Natalie called Mark every night and would get upset if Mark was not available.

Natalie didn't spend a lot of time with her son. Mark's mother took care of Justin as if she was his mother. There were times when she would ask Natalie if it was ok for her to take Justin to visit with her parents. Natalie's response was always the same. She did not want her son around her parents. Mark's mother didn't agree with keeping her grandson from his other grandparents. She secretly did what she could to include Natalie's parents in Justin's life. She sent pictures of Justin and she would often take Justin to their home for visits when Natalie was distracted by school.

Natalie's mother was delighted to find pictures of her grandson in her mailbox and appreciative of those short visits Mark's mother was able to sneak in while Natalie was at school. Natalie's father was never around for the visits. He didn't like the sneaking around, but he was pleased that him wife was happy to spend time with their grandson.

Mark's mother told Mark that she had been taking Justin to visit with Natalie's mother. Mark was glad to hear this but told him mother there was no need to keep it from Natalie. He didn't like hiding it from her.

The next day, Mark told Natalie that his mother had been taking Justin over to visit with her mother. Storming out of the room and dropping the phone to the floor, Natalie went to Mark's mother's room across the hall from hers and threatened to disappear with Justin should it happen again.

Standing in shock and disbelief that Mark had mentioned it to Natalie, she didn't respond to Natalie's threat.

Natalie's behavior became so bizarre that Mark's parents were beginning to worry that Natalie would take the baby and disappear.

During the next few weeks, Natalie became overly friendly and polite towards Mark's parents. She started reading a lot about India. She wanted to know all about what the people were like and what the food was like. She was most intrigued with the city of Mumbai. Mark's mother saw the brochures and pamphlets all about India scattered on the table one day. She was convinced that Natalie was planning to take the baby and run away to India.

"You sure are reading a lot on India. Is this part of a class you are taking?" asked Mark's mother.

"No, just something I decided to read. People are always telling me that I look like I'm from India, so I decided to read up on India to see what the culture was like."

"I can't say I see you as Indian. You are a beautiful girl which is what I'm sure people are noticing. Do you plan on visiting India? I see you have a travel guide in addition to a lot of other information."

"No, not in a million years; I'm just curious about the culture. They have really pretty names there, too. I wish I had known before I named Justin. Some even sound like they could be names of black people. Names like, Priyanka. Priyanka means *"one who is loved"*. Isn't that cool? I bet if I changed my name to an Indian name, I could really pass."

"Why would you want to pass for anything other than what you are? You should take a class in Indian culture if you are that interested in knowing more, but I don't think you should try to pass for anything other than what you are."

"That's a great idea! I will learn so much more from a class. I'm going to look into it. Thanks!"

Mark's mother told her husband of the conversation she had with Natalie and expressed concerned that Natalie was planning to leave with Justin. He told her not to worry because Natalie would never leave knowing that she could not provide for Justin.

Six months after starting her paralegal studies, Natalie received her certificate. She told Mark's parents that she was going to move into her own place once she had a job and had worked enough to save up for an apartment. She spoke no more of a future with Mark. She was angry that Mark had stopped calling her every night. Mark's mother tried to explain to her that Mark was extremely busy with his football schedule.

One morning Mark's parents were awakened by a noise at the door. They walked to the front door to find that the screened door had been blown open by the wind. Knowing that the door was locked each night, they both ran to Natalie's room to see if Natalie and Justin were ok. To their surprise, Natalie and Justin were both missing from their beds. The drawers to the dresser were all left open and emptied. Mark's mother noticed a sheet of paper on the floor. She picked it up and on it Natalie had written in large letters, "NATALIE LIVES HERE NO MORE."

Mark's mother immediately ran to the phone to call 911. She then called Natalie's parents to see if Natalie had decided to move back in with them.

After learning that Natalie had left in the middle of the night, Natalie's parents got dressed and drove over to meet with Mark's parents.

The police were already there when Natalie's parents arrived. Mark's mother was shaken to a point that she could barely speak. Mark's father explained that Natalie had been reading various articles on India and that he feared Natalie may have left the country. The policeman assured him that it was unlikely that she had made it out of the country in such a short time. The policeman went on to explain that Natalie had not committed a crime because there was no custody order in place.

Natalie's parents were scared and embarrassed all at the same time knowing that their daughter had once again proven to be a self-centered person.

The policeman continued to question all four parents to try to understand what could have driven Natalie to the point of running away with the baby. After learning more about Natalie from her parents and Mark's parents, he knew it would be difficult to find Natalie.

Mark's parents called him to let him know that Natalie had run away with Justin. Mark took the first flight home. He was sure that Natalie was just reaching out for attention and would return with an explanation.

Mark was home two days trying to figure out where Natalie had possibly gone with their son. He called all his friends and her friends. No one had seen or heard from Natalie.

After six months had passed with no answers as to where Natalie had disappeared to, the detective handling the case explained to Mark's parents that he was closing the case and suggested that they hire a private detective. Mark's parents did hire a private detective, but he was not successful in finding any traces of Natalie or Justin.

Mark continued to go to school and vowed that one day he was going to find Natalie and his son.

CHAPTER 4

The Proposal

Although Terrance and Priyanka had become inseparable, they managed to keep their relationship professional while at work. There were times when Priyanka would come to Terrance's office for reasons other than work when Harriet had to give Terrance the eye. She felt there was more to their relationship but didn't bother by asking Terrance. She was quite impressed with all the accomplishments Terrance had made in the short time he had been with the firm. She knew that Terrance had a bright future with the firm when she observed his interaction with his boss and other executives. They all spoke highly of Terrance on the monthly conference calls.

Harriet heard others around the office speculating and whispering about the nature of Terrance and Priyanka's relationship. Therefore, she knew it was only a matter of time before Terrance would confide in her.

In addition to their romance, Priyanka was also helpful to Terrance at work. She often provided him with a lot of research on perspective clients. Terrance made it a point to give credit to Priyanka whenever possible.

Barely six months had passed after their first date when Priyanka started asking Terrance to validate their relationship. She wanted to know his expectations? She knew Terrance was in love with her but wanted to know how he felt about marriage. Priyanka was not shy about telling him what she expected from the relationship. She told him in a very direct manner that she did not believe in long-term dating and would not waste her time in a dead-end relationship. Terrance did not take offense to her directness at all. In fact, it was one of the characteristics he loved most about her. He loved not having to guess what she was feeling.

Terrance wanted to marry her but was waiting for more time to pass. He had been talking about marriage to his friends Jaylan and Melody, Jaylan's wife. They both thought it was too soon for him to be talking about marriage with a woman he barely knew. They wanted him to take more time to get to know Priyanka. They had questions about Priyanka's past because she never talked about it. Terrance knew very little about her past. She was vague about her relationship with her family. Whenever anyone asked about her parents, she would find a way to change the subject. It didn't bother Terrance, but it did bother Jaylan and Melody. They wanted to know more about Priyanka and her past.

Struggling with the advice from his friends, Terrance didn't know what to say to Priyanka.

Priyanka waited for a response from Terrance. She saw he was having a difficult time coming up with words to say to her.

"Terrance, I know you are afraid, but you need to stop listening to Jaylan and follow your heart. There are no rules that should dictate when two people know what they feel is real. I love you Terrance, and there is nothing more that I want than to spend the rest of my life loving you."

"My past is painful and not something that I want to share with everyone. I've told you everything that you need to know about my relationship with my parents. Trust me, my family and I didn't write this story. I am not the only person in the world estranged from her family. You do realize, that, right?"

Priyanka looked to Terrance for a sign that he understood her point.

"I understand babe, but you have to understand as well. Jaylan and I have been friends for years, and all I can say to him about your past is that your family left you because they thought you were an embarrassment. To be honest, I've wondered as well. Baby can you tell me more so that I can put this behind us? Why did they consider you an embarrassment?"

"All I can tell you baby is what I have been saying all alone. The story is not going to change because it's the truth. They disowned me a long time ago because in their eyes I was an embarrassment. It was very difficult for me to live by their strict rules."

"What kind of rules baby? I grew up with rules."

Smiling and hesitating before answering Terrance, Priyanka turned and moved closer to face him. She then picked up both of his hands and held them tightly in hers.

"Terrance, you don't understand. My rules were not as simple as clean up your room or make good grades in schools. My rules were more complicated. They chose everything for me like my clothes, my friends, and my food to name a few. As I grew older, I did things my way and started making decisions for myself, but I was never disrespectful. I rebelled by hanging with friends my parents didn't like me around. There was nothing bad about them. They were just different from those I grew up with. My parents found out that I was changing into clothes that I had borrowed from friends when I got to school, and things got even worst when I voiced my opinion to my father."

"And these are the things that caused them to basically throw you away forever?"

"Pretty much and I accepted that a long time ago. I've moved on. I think about them from time to time. There are times when I am angry with them; then, there are times that I'm appreciative because their life style is not for me. I understand their culture, and I doubt that I would be the independent woman that I am today had I followed their rules."

"So, what happened? You woke up one day and they were gone?"

Releasing Terrance's hands and walking away, Priyanka stared out the window.

"No silly, it was not that drastic. I left after graduating high school. I moved in with a friend. We both signed up for classes at City College. After being in college for a few months, I went back home to visit, but my family had moved away and changed their phone number. My friend lost the apartment, so my housing situation got worse. I had no way to reach my parents to let them know, so I moved into a shelter for women. Living in that shelter made me think about a lot of things. I realized that I had disgraced my family, but I'm not one to look back and wish that I had done things differently. I always follow my heart. It's my way of moving forward in life. I finished my two-year degree and never looked back."

Terrance could see that Priyanka was getting emotional. He walked around the table to get to Priyanka as she stood looking out the window. He wiped the tears from her eyes and held her hand and then pulled her closer to him. He held her tightly in his arms. He then pulled back from her and kneeled on one knee.

"I don't have a ring right now, but I want nothing more than to share my life with you. Will you marry me?"

Smiling from ear-to-ear, Priyanka answered yes. Terrance then promised that he would not ask her about her family again because all that mattered was the life that the two of them were starting together.

Priyanka was happy that Terrance had asked for her hand in marriage, but she secretly wished that Terrance would do as she had and leave his family and friends behind. She felt that Terrance had outgrown them, and she was all that he needed to complete his life.

By the end of dinner Priyanka had talked her way into moving in with Terrance. She explained that her apartment lease had run out last month and that she was paying a premium to stay on a month-to-month basis. Terrance agreed that she should move in with him. He promised to have a key made for her the following day so that she could start moving her things by the weekend.

CHAPTER 5

After the Proposal

The day after Terrance proposed to Priyanka was his normal day to have lunch with Jaylan. He called Jaylan to confirm they were still on schedule for lunch because there were times Jaylan would forget to cancel when he was too busy at work to step away. Terrance wanted to be sure Jaylan was going to make it to lunch. He wanted to tell Jaylan about his proposal. But more importantly, he wanted to ask Jaylan not to ask Priyanka anything else about her family or past life.

He wanted Jaylan to finally understand that he was totally committed and happy and wanted nothing more than to marry Priyanka even when he knew very little about her past.

Jaylan confirmed lunch and asked Terrance to meet him at a sandwich shop uptown. Terrance had never been there, so Jaylan had to explain how to get to the restaurant.

Both Jaylan and Terrance arrived at the same time. They sat outside. Jaylan enjoyed people watching. Often, they spent most of their lunch time laughing at Jaylan's jokes about people as they passed the restaurant.

"You sounded like it was mandatory that we have lunch today. What's up? What's on your mind?" asked Jaylan.

"Nothing, well, I shouldn't say nothing because I actually have some good news."

"Let me guess. You've been promoted and given a crazy raise?"

"Man, you're being crazy now. It's nothing like that. I do have something to tell you."

"Wait! You are not about to give me some bad news, are you?"

"Man, just sit back and listen for once in your life."

"Ok. I'm all ears. What's up?"

"Sorry, man. I didn't mean to snap, but I want you to know how serious I am. You know how I feel about Priyanka right?"

"For sure, you love her and probably can't imagine life without her."

"Yes, all of that is true which is why last night I asked her to marry me."

"You did what? That's just foolish man. Why didn't you call me first; or someone before making such a rash decision? Remember, how we talked before I popped the question to my wife? Why so secretive? Better yet, why the rush?"

"Chill man, there was nothing secretive or rushed about it. It was a spur of a moment thing. It just happened. I felt it and went with the feeling. It's no secret how I feel about her. In fact, if it were not for you telling me to give it time, I would have probably proposed to her the day after I met her."

"Yes, I do know that, but I still can't believe it. Have you talked to your mom, dad or anyone else close to you? I just think you are rushing, and I know they will feel the same. I just don't get it; that's all I'm saying. Do you even have a ring? Have you asked her father? Better yet, have you even met her mother or father? Wait, I forgot, they disowned her right? Terrance, you know absolutely nothing about her other than what she wants you to know, and if you ask me, that's shady."

"Are you done? This is the reason I wanted to talk to you face to face. Last night, Priyanka poured her heart out to me talking about her family. I love this girl more than you can probably understand. Everything about her says she is the woman for me. She's smart, intelligent and beautiful. You may not think so, but she is equally in love with me. She is from a different culture--one that we would never understand, and I don't expect you to understand. As a friend, however, I'm asking you not to ask Priyanka about her culture, family or anything that would make her think of her past. I'm not asking; I'm insisting on it, no more questions. She will tell us more when she is ready. She did confide in me that it makes her very sad and uncomfortable whenever you ask her about her parents. She is going to be my wife and the mother of my children. Do you get where I'm coming from?"

"I do get where you are coming from, and I say this with mad respect for you. There is something about her that does not feel right to me, man. I get the whole culture differences, but you must ask yourself why she can't answer the simple questions. Why are the simple questions so painful, and where are her friends? With all, out of respect for you I will not speak to her about her culture, past or parents. However, ask yourself some of those simple questions, like where did she grow up? What schools did she attend? Who are her friends? Has she ever been married?"

"Listen, Jaylan, just drop it. Trust that I have everything under control. Priyanka is a good woman, and I'm lucky to have her and lucky that she wants to marry me. I'm the who should be thankful one in this equation. All I need from you is your support. We have been friends too long to let this become an issue between us."

Just as Jaylan was about to respond, he saw that Terrance had become distracted.

"What's going on? I was about to say something to you, but I guess you have your mind set."

"I do, but I thought I just saw someone I used to know."

"Who did you see?"

"Charlene."

"Who is Charlene?"

"She's from my old neighborhood. You didn't know her. She and her mother moved out of the neighborhood before I went to high school. That can't be her, though. What are the chances of running into her here in New York?"

"I don't think I've ever heard you mention her in all the years that I've known you."

"I know. I kind of forgot about her myself. She was friends with Latonja, but once she and her mother moved out of the neighborhood, we never heard from them again. Now that I think about it, I did ask Latonja about her. I almost forgot. She said she heard that Charlene was living on the east coast somewhere. I believe she said Philly."

"I didn't see her, but we should go look for her. She may just be Charlene," offered Jaylan

"Nawl, it was probably just a resemblance. Besides, that girl was fine. I have a less than fine memory of Charlene."

"How fine could she have been at twelve?" replied Jaylan.

Both men looked at each other and laughed after Jaylan's statement. It was a nice break from the heated discussion about Priyanka.

"I am happy for you man. I want the best for you and Priyanka. If truth be known, I knew you were going to marry her. I just didn't know it was going to be so soon."

"Let's all get together this weekend to celebrate, and before I forget, I need your help with moving Priyanka to my place."

"Oh, she's moving in too?"

"Yes, we decided it would be best. She's paying way too much for a month-to-month lease on her apartment."

"No problem; just tell me when and where to report."

"Thanks man, I better get back to the office. I'll talk to you later," replied Terrance.

Terrance and Jaylan walked back to their cars in opposite directions. Jaylan was still trying to process the conversation he had about Priyanka being uncomfortable talking about her past. He was sure to mention to his wife not to ask Priyanka about her past. Terrance still had the image in his head of the woman he believed to be Charlene.

CHAPTER 6

The Announcement

Terrance was relieved that he had spoken to Jaylan about Priyanka and left feeling that Jaylan had understood. He told Priyanka about his conversation with Jaylan and assured her that Jaylan would not question her about her past. Priyanka didn't feel any comfort in what she was told by Terrance because she knew the attorney in Jaylan was bound to resurface and start to dig into her past.

Priyanka wanted to make an announcement in the office about their engagement, but Terrance wanted them to have a conversation with his parents first because he had not told them about his engagement. Priyanka had totally forgotten about his parents. She apologized and blamed it on being overly excited.

"We should call my parents tonight."

"Sounds good, baby, and then we can tell everyone in the office."

"No, I think we should wait a little while longer before we say anything to anyone in the office."

"If you say so, but I'm so excited about life with you that I can barely contain myself. I want to scream out loud to the world that I'm going to be Mrs. Priyanka Johnson."

"Please don't baby. We are in the office."

Priyanka smiled and added distance between the two of them.

"Do you think your mother will be ok with us --especially after she learns that I'm moving in with you before we are actually married? You know how she is, Baby, with her southern ways."

"Don't be critical of my mother. She just respects the sanctity of marriage, but ultimately what we do is our personal choice. She will be more shocked to hear about our engagement than anything else simply because she has never met you in person. Don't worry about my mother. She has always had my back regardless of whether or not she agrees with my choices."

"Baby, I would never criticize your mother. How could I? She brought a wonderful, handsome, strong and sexy man into this world just for me." Moving closer, Priyanka kissed Terrance on the lips.

Gently moving his lips away, "Baby, did you forget we are in the office? We better get back to work before we both are in trouble."

Slowly walking backwards out of the office, Priyanka waved and whispered, "I'll see you later."

Terrance had promised his parents that he and Priyanka were going to call them after work, but he did not tell them why they were calling. His mother suspected that they were calling to announce their engagement based on her conversation with Terrance. He asked his mother to talk to Priyanka but not to ask her any questions about her family.

"Ok, I won't ask her about her family. You must have a good reason, so I won't ask you why. Your father and I will talk to you later."

His parents had been asking Terrance to bring Priyanka to Alabama to meet them, but Terrance would always make up an excuse. He felt Priyanka was not ready to meet his family based on her negative views of the South and people who she felt were underachievers. Terrance believed Priyanka's negative views were based on her not having a family and that her views would change once she became a part of his family.

"Hey Mom, I have you on speaker phone so that Priyanka and I both can talk to you.

"Ok. I wish your dad were here to talk, too. He just left for the store. Hey Priyanka, how you doing?"

"Hi, Mrs. Johnson, I'm doing well. How are you?"

"I can't complain. When y'all coming up here to see us? We have been dying to meet you. All Terrance talks about whenever he calls home is you."

"We will visit soon, right Terrance?" asked Priyanka attempting to turn the conversation back over to Terrance.

"Yeah Mom, we will be there sooner than you think. Actually, there is a reason we are calling tonight."

"What might that be?"

"Well, Mom, as you know, I am crazy in love with Priyanka."

"Yes, that I do know."

"Well, Mom, I've asked her to marry me, and she has said yes. We wanted you to hear it from the two of us. What do you think?"

"You sound nervous. You've said "well, Mom" I don't know how many times. You know I'm always happy for you and will support your decisions. If there's one thing your dad and I have always taught you is that you have to make your own decisions and live by them. I know you must love her because you talk about her all the time. Priyanka, no one can say that my son does not love you. I just pray that you love him equally. If so, then I'm happy for both of y'all. Just keep God first is my only advice. Will y'all be getting married up there?"

"Thank you, Mrs. Johnson, your blessing means a lot to me. And don't worry, I love Terrance just as much, if not more."

"I like hearing you say that because we raised our son to be a good man and want him to have a good wife--one who will treat him like a king."

Priyanka was somewhat speechless, after Mrs. Johnson referred to her son as a king. She thought it was a backward statement and something that an uneducated person would say, therefore she smiled, looking over at Terrance, and remained quiet. Terrance ended the call by saying good night to his mother and telling her that he loved her.

"Now that was not, hard, was it?"

"No baby, it was not. Your mother is a kind lady. I can see where your kindness comes from.

CHAPTER 7

Moving Day

Terrance wanted to be sure Priyanka was moved into his apartment before he went to Alabama.

Jaylan and a few other friends of Terrance's had agreed to help with moving Priyanka's things into Terrance's apartment. Most of Priyanka's furniture was taken to a storage unit. It was things like her clothes, shoes and other personal belongings that had to be moved to Terrance's apartment. Although most of her furniture was placed in storage, she did have a few pieces she wanted to take with her, like her favorite chair. She wanted it in the bedroom that she would share with Terrance. She also had a few pieces moved into the spare room.

There was one box made of hard plastic about the size of a shoebox that Priyanka kept close to her. Jaylan reached for the box as he was moving other things, but Priyanka immediately stepped in front of him to let him know that she was taking care of that particular box.

Jaylan didn't question her because he remembered the conversation he had with Terrance. He did, however, watch closely, from a distance, to see where she placed the box in the closet. He didn't know when or how he was going to find out what was in the box, but he was going to try. He could tell from Priyanka's reaction when he reached for the box that there was something in the box that she didn't want anyone to know about. Priyanka didn't notice Jaylan watching as she placed the box in the far corner on the closet floor.

CHAPTER 8

Office Announcement

Terrance and Harriet arrived at the office thirty minutes before anyone else as they normally do each day. He told Harriet that he had proposed to Priyanka. He wanted her to be the first in the office to know.

"Really?"

"Yes, are you surprised? I know we've kept our relationship away from the office, but I was sure if anyone in the office knew, it would be you."

Harriet didn't say what was on her mind. Terrance felt relieved that Harriet didn't have a negative reaction. He thought she was going to lecture him on how it was too soon, but instead, she surprised him with a blessing. Of course, Harriet did not approve, but she was a couple of years away from retirement and didn't want to say anything to jeopardize her retirement. She had developed an almost mother-to-son relationship with Terrance, but she didn't know how he would react if she expressed her true feelings. She knew the day was coming as she watched Priyanka put her moves on Terrance but didn't' feel she knew enough about Priyanka outside of work to offer any advice even when she felt Terrance should have given it more time. There was something about Priyanka that she didn't trust. One day while passing Priyanka's desk, she noticed a recipe on Priyanka's computer screen. She stopped momentarily to get a closer looker. A few days later, Priyanka brought the dish to the office to share. She received many compliments. It was not until her response to someone who asked for the recipe that confirmed to Harriet that Priyanka was a liar and was hiding something. Priyanka told the person that it was a secret family recipe from her mother and it was the last thing that she was holding onto from her past. Harriet was outspoken, but she refused to get involved in matters of the heart. Her retirement was her priority.

Thirty minutes later, Priyanka came to the office with two dozen glazed donuts, a gallon of coffee and a big smile on her face. Priyanka always came to the office dressed well, but she had purchased a new outfit just to wear to the office on the day she decided she was going to announce her engagement to Terrance. Terrance was a little shocked to see all that Priyanka had gone through just to tell a few people about their engagement. He had only agreed to Priyanka's casually telling a few people. He didn't know how to react to the company-wide e-mail that Priyanka sent out minutes after signing on to her computer. The e-mail asked employees to report to the conference room for a brief meeting.

Smiling, Priyanka watched employees as they gathered in the conference room, each reaching for a donut as they wondered what the meeting was about. Most assumed there was going to be a major announcement regarding the firm. Priyanka motioned for Terrance to join her at the front of the room. Hesitantly Terrance slowly walked to the front of the room to join Priyanka. He looked to his left to see Harriet standing there with a perplexed look on her face and folded arms.

"May I have your attention everyone?" shouted Priyanka to get the attention of the employees.

The room went completely silent and all attention was on Terrance and Priyanka. Priyanka was as excited as a child at Christmas about to open her first present, and Terrance was as stiff as a child about to give his first Easter speech.

"I know that most of you, if not all of you, are probably wondering why Terrance and I are standing here in front of you. First let me say, we are not here to talk about a bonus or any changes within the firm, so you all can relax."

Immediately, the noise level increased as employees started to talk amongst themselves. They wanted to know what was going on, and why a meeting was called if there was nothing to announce about the company.

"Everyone please be patient with me!"

The noise level decreased, but some people were still talking. Priyanka knew she could not make her announcement as she had planned because she could see that some people were annoyed.

"Ok, I can see you all are becoming quite impatient, so I'll get to the point. Terrence and I have something much more fantastic to announce than a bonus or any changes within the firm. Everyone buckle your seat belts! Terrance has asked me to marry him! And I said yes!"

It was at the moment of dead silence and no reaction to Priyanka's announcement that Terrance decided to step in and add his comments. He could see from the expressions of the people in the room as he took a quick scan that people were outraged that their day had been interrupted for something not work related. He, himself, was relieved that his boss had taken the week off and was not there to witness Priyanka's announcement.

"Good morning everyone! What's up with the silence? I know you all are shocked to say the least, but Priyanka and I thought we would share our good news with you good folks over donuts and coffee. Please accept my apology if we somehow interrupted your day, but since you all are already here, please enjoy donuts and coffee on us."

Smiling apologetically, Terrance could see that people had a different reaction to him. The tension in the room almost immediately subsided, and people started to walk up to him and Priyanka to congratulate them.

Later that night Terrance talked with Priyanka over dinner.

"Baby, I wish you had come to me before planning to make an announcement in the office about our engagement."

"I did tell you. What's the problem? Are you ashamed or something?"

"No, that's not it at all and I thought you were just going to tell people informally. You know, a few people, not the entire office. I would have preferred it if you had kept it on a much smaller scale, like one-on-one."

"What's the difference?" she asked.

"Well, it came across as unprofessional. I'm actually glad my boss was away. We just have to be careful baby and keep things professional at work."

"Terrance, I'm tired and don't feel like eating much. I thought I was doing a good thing, but I guess not."

Priyanka left the room and headed upstairs. Terrance knew she was upset but felt he had to let her know how he felt about the situation.

The following morning Terrance was awakened by the smell of bacon and blueberry pancakes. He walked to the kitchen to find Priyanka preparing breakfast.

"Looks who's up bright and early this morning," remarked Terrance as he greeted Priyanka with a kiss.

"I feel bad, Terrance, for my behavior last night. I know you meant well. I behaved like a child by not having dinner and going to bed, so I wanted to make it up to you with these hot and fluffy pancakes and crispy bacon."

Moving closer to Terrance with a plate resting on the palm of her hand, she kissed him on the lips before resting the plate on the table.

"Baby, I don't want us to ever go to bed angry. Promise me that we can talk about anything and work it out before going to bed," stated Terrance.

"I promise Terrance. It won't happen again. I don't know what came over me. I was just excited to let everyone know that very soon I will be Mrs. Priyanka Johnson. Doesn't that sound good, Baby?"

"Yes, it does, and I understand your excitement. Keep in mind, though, we have to remain professional at the office. I'm sure some people were happy about the announcement, but as I looked around the room I could see that some people were annoyed. In all honestly most companies frown upon office romances because it could present all types of problems. I know that won't be the case with us, but we have to keep it professional."

"I'm sorry Baby. I promise, you won't even know I'm in the office starting today."

CHAPTER 9

Wedding Plan

F inding a wedding planner was an easy task for Priyanka. The firm once represented a client who was a wedding planner. Priyanka remembered having a conversation with the owner as she waited to be seen by the attorney handling her case. The owner had an interesting story. She was there to sue a client, who happened to be her own father, for non-payment of services. Flipping through the calendar of the previous year, Priyanka found the person she was looking for. She called and spoke to the women for twenty minutes. The woman remembered her and offered her a substantial discount because she recalled Priyanka being kind and understanding and not judging her for suing her father. Priyanka scheduled a face-to-face meeting with her the next day.

Priyanka had taken the next day off to meet with the wedding planner and had indicated to Terrance that she was going to stop by the office to meet him for lunch if she finished with the planner in time.

The meeting with the planner went well and was productive. August 18th was set as their wedding date. Priyanka and Terrance had exactly six months to prepare for their special day.

Priyanka decided to stop by the office to see if Terrance could slip away for lunch despite it's being two hours past lunch-time. She was sure that Terrance would not mind and would make time for her, no matter what he was doing.

Priyanka stepped into Terrance's office, but he was not there. She walked around the corner to see if Harriet knew whether he was in the office or off meeting with a client. Harriet told her to check the break room because she knew he had not left the office. When Priyanka entered the break room she saw Terrance talking to a couple of female co-workers. Terrance had no idea that Priyanka had entered the room because his back was facing the entrance to the room. His co-workers were facing the entrance and could see Priyanka as she entered the room. The expression on her face said to them that she was not happy to find Terrance talking to them although the conversation was innocent and mostly about his engagement.

"Hi Priyanka, I thought you were out today. Terrance was just telling us you were meeting with a wedding planner," stated one of the co-workers.

While glaring at Terrance as if he had committed a crime and without taking her eyes off him, Priyanka, replied, "Yes, I was meeting with our wedding planner."

"Hey, I didn't expect to see you here after I didn't hear from you earlier. How did it go with the planner?" asked Terrance attempting to ease the tension he was feeling from Priyanka.

"I see. I'm sure you didn't expect to see me. Why didn't you call me if you had not heard from me? Anything could have happened to me while you were busy spending time in the break room socializing," replied Priyanka as if she had caught Terrance doing something wrong.

The two co-workers could see that Terrance was embarrassed. They were even embarrassed for him, so they congratulated Priyanka again and quietly left the room with thoughts that Priyanka was out-of-line.

"What has gotten into you Priyanka? That was rude and embarrassing to say the least. I can't even talk to you right now, but we must talk about this later. I'll see you later." Terrance, obviously upset, left the room without looking back at Priyanka.

Terrance drove home thinking of what he was going to say to Priyanka and trying to understand why she behaved the way she had. He questioned whether or not her behavior was indicative of her true personality. He would have never imagined that she would be insecure about him being around other women in the office. His mind started to recall how she made the announcement in the office without consulting him, and he wondered if this was a sign of her insecurity. He thought of calling Jaylan to vent but didn't want to arouse Jaylan's doubts about Priyanka.

Terrance could hear music playing as he put the key in the door to his apartment. He opened the door to find Priyanka standing in a white revealing nightshirt holding a glass of champagne in each of her hands. The music was soft and romantic, and candles were lit throughout the room.

Terrance quickly forgot that he was disappointed with Priyanka's behavior earlier in the office. It didn't take him long to decide that he was not going to say anything for fear of spoiling the romantic moment Priyanka had created. He accepted her gesture as an unspoken apology.

The next morning, just as Priyanka had predicted, Terrance said nothing of the incident. She prepared breakfast as usual and started talking about the wedding as if she had not embarrassed Terrance the day before.

CHAPTER 10

Who's That Girl

Terrance and Jaylan planned to meet for lunch at the same sandwich shop where they last had lunch. Terrance had every intention of venting to Jaylan about the announcement Priyanka had made in the office and the way she acted towards his co-workers the previous week, but he decided against it since he and Priyanka had gotten past it.

Terrance had been sitting at the restaurant waiting on Jaylan for fifteen minutes when he received a call from Jaylan letting him know that he was not going to make it to lunch because he was still in court with his client. He told Terrance that he would catch up with him later at the gym.

Terrance's first thought was to leave the area, but he decided to work on some contracts he had with him. He looked across the street and saw there was an office building. He decided not to have lunch and to walk over to the building to see if there was a quiet place where he could work on his contracts. As Terrance gathered his things, he noticed the same woman he had seen a month prior, when he was last in the area with Jaylan.

Terrance almost stepped into traffic without looking while trying to get a closer view of the woman. By the time he entered the building he saw the woman enter, she was nowhere in sight, but there was a small lounge area with a big-screen TV where Terrance could work on his contracts. The TV was tuned in to CNN where there was much conversation about the OJ Simpson case. Terrance was not interested, so he tuned it out and worked on his contracts. Terrance was so focused on what he was doing that he did not notice that more than ten people had gathered around the

TV watching intensely while waiting on a verdict. He turned to look up at the TV to see what was going on. It was then that he realized that it was the day of the verdict in the OJ Simpson case. At that moment, he felt that the world had stopped, and everyone wanted to know the fate of OJ Simpson. He could hear various conversations around him, all of which seemed to lean towards the idea that OJ was guilty. As the judge asked the jury if they had reached a verdict and the answer was "yes", everyone stood stiffly as though they were holding their breath and were almost out of air. As the "not guilty" verdict was read, there was a sigh of release and disappointment, all at the same time. It was not until then that Terrance turned to look at the people around him. Everyone behind him was clearly upset about the verdict. Terrance picked up his things to leave without making direct eye contact with anyone because the few glimpses he caught made him feel as though he had committed the crime. He felt that many people had allowed the media to turn the OJ Simpson case into a racial case. Terrance felt that race had no place in the matter, and he felt that OJ Simpson was guilty. He knew those people standing around him believed he felt otherwise. Terrance continued to find his way past the people in the lounge area while keeping his head as low as possible.

When he looked up momentarily, he saw the woman he was trying to reach earlier. She, too, was trying to make her way out of the lounge area.

"Charlene?" called Terrance as he got close enough to the woman to say something to her.

Surprised to hear someone call her name, she stopped walking and turned to see if she had in fact heard someone call out to her.

"Oh, my goodness! Is that you, all grown up Terrance?"

"Yes, it's me, and I can't believe it's you. What are you doing here? Do you live here? Stand back and let me look at you! Terrance stood back to get a full view of Charlene. You look good girl!"

"Terrance, you are too funny. Give me a hug boy! It's so good to see you! Oh, my goodness! Not in a million years would I have thought that I would run into you here in New York. As a matter of fact, I never thought I would run into you anywhere. Do you live here? Wait! Do you have to be somewhere, or do you have a few minutes? I want to catch up as much as possible. My flight doesn't leave for a few hours, so I have a few minutes.

I was actually on my way to the airport to just sit around and wait for my flight."

"Are you hungry?' asked Terrance

"Sort of, I guess I can eat something light."

"Good, I know the perfect little sandwich shop across the street."

"I'm still pinching myself. Not in a million years," Charlene repeated, as she sat next to Terrance at the table.

"You won't believe this, but I was only out here to meet a friend for lunch. He couldn't make it out of court, which is why I was over in that building working on a few contracts. Talk about fate."

"Did you say court?"

"Yes, he's an attorney like myself."

"Terrance, I apologize. I just heard court and I assumed the worst."

"No need to apologize, I understand. I would probably have made the same assumption."

"Can you believe that verdict in the OJ case?" asked Charlene.

"No, I can't. I think he did it, or he arranged it. I guess we'll never know, though Based on the ugly looks I got when the verdict was read, you would have thought I was a character witness for OJ. It's all so crazy to me," replied Terrance

"I know. I received some nasty looks too, but who cares. I just think the media played a role into turning this whole thing into a race issue. I honestly think that most black people believe that OJ is guilty. I think, however, that they feel some sense of justice in knowing that a black man got off for once when so many black men have been falsely accused and incarcerated for years for something they didn't do. I recently heard of a case where a black man was released from jail after spending twenty years of his life incarcerated for something he did not do," stated Charlene.

"I totally agree. I could not have said it better myself. What do you do for a living, Charlene? And how's your mother?"

"I'm a sales manager for a software company. My sales district is here and in surrounding states. I've been coming back and forth here for about three months now. My client is about to go live with our software product, so I don't have much time left here."

"Sounds like you, running things. I'm just glad to see you. Who would have guessed that we would run into each other here in New York City? And your mother, how's she?"

Charlene pausing for a moment answered, "My mom died before I finished high school. She worked so hard and spent most of her life trying to do better for me. She died before she really got a chance to enjoy life. Remember those long hours she spent at school when I had to stay with you and your family until she got home?" Charlene smiled as she spoke of those days.

"Are you kidding me? How could I forget? I know you hated staying over. You thought you were grown enough to stay home alone."

"I did, but Mama wasn't having it. Anyway, she became ill and died suddenly, only an hour after making it to the emergency room. She was only thirty- three years old, Terrance. She was an amazing mother and a great influence on my life."

"I'm sorry to hear that, Charlene. She was an amazing lady, and you were blessed to have her as your mother."

"I am blessed to have had her as my mother, but I will say that after losing her, it was a sad and crazy time for me. My world was turned upside down the day that my mother died. She was my best friend, Terrance. I wanted to make her proud because she had done so much to make life better for me. She was a single mom making things happen for us and I always felt her love. It was hard for me to imagine life without her because I didn't feel anyone cared about me as she had. She was my biggest cheerleader. To be honest, I still feel there's no replacement for a mother's love of her child. There was no one left in my world for me to make proud of me, but I had to find strength to keep pushing forward. I had to move to Philadelphia to live with my father's sister. It was strange because I had never even met her. My father, who I barely knew was in no position to take me in. It was his fault that I didn't know any of my relatives on his side of the family. My aunt was good to me and tried hard to make up for the time she didn't know me. In the beginning, she tried to fill Mama's shoes, but it wasn't happening. We clashed a lot until she found another way to reach me."

"I hear you. Did you ever find out what was wrong with your mother?"

"Oh, I apologize. We did find out. She had a blood clot. If you remember, my mother was slim. I mean skinny. Mama was really skinny." Charlene laughed out loud as she thought of how small her mother was. "It does not matter how slim you are. It's a matter of taking care of yourself by visiting your doctor on an annual basis to determine if there is a problem. Mama had a blood clot in her leg that she didn't know about. Ultimately, it led to a heart attack. That's why I'm very conscientious about what I eat, and I'm an advocate for healthy eating and exercise."

"I hear you. I'm just happy to see that you are doing well. I feel your mom is looking down and is one very proud mama."

"Thanks T. So, what's up with you? I see you still have that caring characteristic about yourself. How's life treating you as an attorney? Or do you call yourself a lawyer?" Throwing her hands up in the air and laughing out loud, Charlene leaned forward and reached to touch Terrance's hand. "It really is good to see you, Terrance."

Leaning forward and responding to her touch with his hand. "It's nice to see you, too." Terrance quickly moved his hand back when he felt a tingling as he looked into her eyes.

"To answer your question, attorney, lawyer, it does not matter, but life is really good. I have no complaints."

"Well, Mr. Lawyer, I don't see a ring on your finger, and you have not pulled out any pictures. I'm guessing you are not married?"

"No, I'm not, but I'm happy to say that I'm engaged to a beautiful, hot woman."

Charlene reacted to Terrance's words as if someone had poured cold water on her. Her demeanor went from hot and flirty to friendly and concerned.

"You had to throw in the "hot, so typical, so typical. Shaking her head and laughing, Charlene reached for the glass of water on the table in front of her and took a sip. "That's so sweet to hear you speak of her like that, though I can see you are really in love. Maybe, I'll get to meet her one day."

"You will, without a doubt. You'll like her too. What about you? I don't see a ring on your finger either."

"That's because I have not been as lucky as you have in the love department, but I'm working on it." Laughing and reaching for the glass, she took another sip of water.

"So, what else is new in your world, Terrance? Have you been back to Alabama lately?"

"Actually, I was there recently. I take it that you don't know about Pookie?"

"No. What about him?"

"I'll spare you the details, but he passed; someone actually killed him. I lost contact with him over the years and although he chose a different path in life from me, he was a pretty good guy. He and Latonja were there for each other. I learned recently from Latonja how much the two of them were in love. They had a bond that no one could question. They have three boys who are just as full of life as Latonja and Pookie were when we were kids."

"Wow, I had no idea."

"I was there a few months ago to help Latonja get things in order for herself and her children. And before then I had a chance to sit with Pookie in the hospital before he passed. He had my mother to ask me to come to visit him. He had to have known he was dying. He wanted to talk to me. Can you believe it? He talked about Troy a little. He still carried guilt over Troy's death after all these years. He said that Latonja helped him to accept that he was not at fault. There was so much to Pookie. I know he would have chosen a different path had he been dealt a different hand in life. Man, what I would not give just to live a few moments in that time. I would say so much to him to encourage him. We had very little, yet so much that we didn't appreciate at the time."

"That's life, Terrance. Time moves on. We all have to live by our choices; but it was really nice of you to take the time to visit with him. He was a pretty cool guy. You'll have to give Latonja my number. I would love to speak to her."

"I'm sure she would like that too."

Sitting back in her chair to take it all in, Charlene reached in her purse for her phone to check the time.

Looking down at his phone on the table, Terrance could see that he had several missed calls from Priyanka.

"Charlene, I am so sorry; time has flown by, and I have to get back to the office." Passing her a pen and paper before getting up from the table, Terrance asked Charlene to write down her number. "I'll call you later."

"Sure, but are you ok? You seem worried."

"No, I just can't believe how much time has passed."

"It has, but it was really good chatting and catching up with you. I hope to hear from you soon."

"It was good seeing you too, Charlene, and I promise to be in touch. I can't wait for you to meet my finance'."

Terrance and Charlene hugged as they left each other. Terrance was distracted by the fact that he had missed several calls from Priyanka. He called Priyanka's desk as soon as he reached his car, but his call was placed on hold for several minutes. He decided to hang up and deal with Priyanka when he returned to the office.

Terrance returned, and it didn't appear that anyone had been looking for him. He was even greeted by Priyanka. Priyanka had assumed that Terrance and Jaylan were having an extended lunch as they have done from time to time. She was not at all concerned about the missed calls.

"Baby, you would not believe the day I had today."

"Really, anything special happen?"

"I was supposed to meet Jaylan."

"Wait, you mean you didn't?" she interrupted.

"Right, he didn't show up because he was in court with his client. I ended up going across the street to an office building to finish some work. I didn't get a whole lot done because of watching the OJ verdict. You would not believe the looks I got when that verdict was read. You would have thought I was Johnny Cochran."

"Then that explains the long lunch. I heard the verdict as well. It was on in the break room. People were talking about a group of African American students at some college celebrating after the verdict was read. It's sad is all I can say. I really don't have an opinion, so I avoided all of those conversations."

"Good for you but the crazy thing that happened was that I ran into a friend from my old neighborhood."

"Really, who in the world would you have run into from Alabama?"

"Her name is Charlene. I don't think that I've ever mentioned her to you. She moved away from our neighborhood before high school."

"Correct. I've never heard of Charlene. How exactly did you run into her?"

Terrance paused for a moment because he could tell that Priyanka didn't trust what he was saying.

"She was in the building that I went to. She was there for her job, but like everyone else she was watching the verdict. Most people were only passing by and stopped to see what everyone else was watching. I ran into her on my way out of the building. She was in town on business. She has a customer located in that building. I thought I saw her a month ago when I was last there having lunch with Jaylan, but I didn't think twice about it. She had to leave to catch her flight back home to Pennsylvania, but I have her number. I want you to meet her the next time she's in town."

"How did you even know about the restaurant?"

"Jaylan, and it's really a small sandwich shop. He knows all the good restaurants, even those uptown."

Priyanka could see that Terrance was feeling her jealous vibe, so she decided to back off with her questions. She knew she would meet Charlene and would determine then if Charlene would become an issue in her relationship with Terrance.

"I'm meeting Jaylan at the gym since we didn't meet today."

"Good idea since he didn't show up for lunch. When should I expect you back?"

"I'll be back in about two hours. Do you want me to pick up dinner?"

"That would be great, your choice."

While heading to the gym, Terrance went back and forth with deciding whether to talk to Jaylan about his concerns regarding Priyanka.

As soon as he reached Jaylan at the gym he started talking about Charlene and how he ran into her near the restaurant.

Jaylan was happy to see that Terrance was excited, but he knew that Charlene would not be a threat to Priyanka because he knew how much Terrance was in love. Not even someone from his old neighborhood could break the spell he was under when it came to Priyanka. On the other hand, he knew Priyanka would not be happy because she wanted Terrance to forget about his past life in Alabama.

CHAPTER 11

What Was That About?

J aylan was at his favorite sandwich shop without Terrance when he
noticed a woman across the street clearly in distress trying to get
away from a man. At first glance, he thought it was a couple having a
disagreement and he didn't want to get involved. When he took a second
glance, however, he noticed that it was Priyanka. He immediately ran
across the street to see what was going on.

"Priyanka! Priyanka!" he called out as he ran towards her.

The man was holding her arm and trying to get her to talk to him as
she tried pulling away, but he held on tight until Jaylan made his way close
enough to defend Priyanka.

"What's going on here? What's your business with her?" Looking away
from the scared stranger and over at Priyanka. "Priyanka, who is this and
what's going on?"

"Jaylan, let's just go. I don't know this man. He thought I was someone
else. I have no clue why he felt a need to try to force me into saying I'm a
person that I'm not," replied Priyanka as she looked at the stranger as if
she was daring him to disagree with her.

"Dude, I'm sorry. I honestly thought she was someone else--someone I
knew a long time ago and someone who has been missing for years," replied
the stranger. He gave Priyanka an equally puzzling look as if to say that
she had not heard the last of him.

"Jaylan, please, let it go. It's ok. There's not a problem. Clearly he was
mistaken."

"You really need to watch yourself, man. You can't go around trying to force people to talk to you against their will. She could have you arrested. You damn lucky she wants to drop it all."

"Dude, I said I'm sorry to you both. I hear everything that you are saying. I got the message loud and clear. Now, if you don't mind I'm going about my business. Good day to you both," replied the stranger as he walked away leaving Jaylan and Priyanka standing as they watched him walk away.

"That was strange. Are you ok? If I had not known better, I would have thought the two of you knew each other."

"Jaylan, you heard the man. He was mistaken, and please don't scare Terrance about this nonsense. I do thank you for coming to my defense. I was having a difficult time trying to convince him that I was not who he thought I was."

"Did he call you a certain name?" asked Jaylan.

"I'm not sure. Why are you so curious about a stranger?"

"I'm not, it was just all so strange to me. Why are you all the way up here?"

"I'm here shopping for my wedding dress. The wedding planner sent me here. A better question is why are you here?"

"I come here for lunch often. There's a cool little sandwich shop up here.

"Oh, is that where you and Terrance have lunch from time to time--the place where he ran into Charlene?"

"Yes. Listen, I'm not going to alarm Terrance, but I think he should know what happened here today."

"I agree. I'll just make sure that I don't ever come here alone again."

"Good idea. Do you want to grab a bite to eat before you go back to the office since you're here?"

"No, but thanks for asking. I've lost the little appetite that I had."

Jaylan didn't know what to make of what he witnessed with Priyanka and the stranger, but he felt that he was being misled by Priyanka. He thought of the box that Priyanka was hiding in her closet. He wondered if he could find answers in that box to understand Priyanka.

Later that evening, Jaylan called Terrance to tell him about the incident. Terrance told Jaylan that Priyanka had told him all about what had happened and that she promised him that she would not go back alone.

Jaylan didn't pursue the issue because he knew it would only upset Terrance.

CHAPTER 12

Jaylan and Melody

Jaylan ended the conversation with Terrance, confused and a little upset that Terrance didn't ask more about what he had told him he witnessed with Priyanka and the stranger. He sat across the dinner table from his wife, Melody, wondering if he should have said more.

"What's wrong, Jay? Did you have a rough day at the office or something?"

"No, but the strangest thing happened today with Priyanka."

"Here we go again. If I didn't know better, I'd say you had a little crush on her. What are you suspicious about now?"

"I ran into her today uptown."

"Jay, there's no crime in that. Did you forget about the promise you made to Terrance? I think you should let it go and trust that he knows what he is doing when it concerns Priyanka. If the tables were turned, you would not appreciate it, so just let it go."

"I hear what you are saying, and I was there. What I witnessed today placed me right back where I started. Baby, I'm telling you Priyanka is hiding something."

Cutting her steak, Melody stopped for a moment to give Jaylan her undivided attention.

"Ok, I'll ask. What happened today with her?"

"I was about to have lunch when I saw this man pulling on this woman's arm. When I looked closer, I noticed that it was Priyanka's arm this stranger was pulling on."

"Really? What the hell? Don't stop now. I have to hear this."

"To make a long story short, I had to run over to get this man to release her arm. Apparently, he thought she was someone else but, Baby, they gave each other a look that seemed as if they knew each other. I just happened to be there to interrupt whatever disagreement they were having."

"Stop! Are you being serious?"

"I'm as serious as they come, and Terrance didn't seem bothered by it. I guess he trusts that Priyanka won't go there alone again. She told him she was there to meet the wedding planner to look at wedding dresses."

"I agree with you; it does sound fishy,- but it's none of our business. Did she say exactly where she was meeting the wedding planner? I can't imagine her going to look at wedding dresses alone with the wedding planner, but I could be wrong. Like I said, it's none of our business." Melody stood and walked towards the sink to rinse her plate. "I'm telling you, Jay, stay out of it."

Still sitting at the table and looking over his shoulder at Melody, Jaylan replied, "I hear you. I'll stay out of it."

CHAPTER 13

Priyanka Meets Charlene

Terrance had arranged for Charlene to be picked up from the hotel and brought to his apartment to meet him and Priyanka for dinner. Priyanka was more than eager to meet Charlene. Charlene wanted to meet somewhere close to her hotel, but Priyanka insisted that Terrance send a car for her so the three of them could ride to the restaurant together.

When the doorbell rang, Priyanka was still in the bathroom prepping to look her very best for Charlene. Terrance went to answer the door. Terrance was speechless when he opened the door to see Charlene standing there in five feet eight inches tall wearing a form fitting multi-colored dress and sling back 4-inch heels and waiting for an invitation to step into the house.

"Wow!"

Charlene smiled at Terrance's reaction to her.

Terrance no longer saw her as the slim girl from his childhood neighborhood with thick glasses and long ponytails on each side of her head. There she stood before him with long silky black hair, big beautiful brown eyes not hidden by thick glasses and though Charlene was still very slim, she had a curvy figure.

"Terrance, don't just stand there, let our guest in," stated Priyanka as she silently walked behind Terrance and watched as he stood clearly stunned by Charlene's beauty.

"Come on in Charlene," replied Terrance.

"Thank you for coming," stated Priyanka.

"Thank you for having me.

"Charlene, this is my beautiful future wife, Priyanka," Terrance stated, as Charlene stepped into the house.

"I figured as much, and she is even more beautiful than you described."

"You're kind," replied Priyanka.

Priyanka extended her hand for a handshake, but Charlene gave her a hug instead. "Girl, come here, I prefer a hug over a handshake." Priyanka smiled and laughed it off as if she was not annoyed by Charlene's comment.

"Priyanka is such a beautiful name. Does your name have a special meaning?"

"Priyanka is from Mumbai, India, and her name means "one who is loved," explained Terrance

"I see. That's so special. I don't think my name means anything. I'll have to look it up one day," replied Charlene jokingly.

"All the names in your culture means something, right Baby?" asked Terrance attempting to engage her in conversation.

"Yes, all the names mean something. I've never looked up the meaning of my name, but my parents would always tell me that it meant that I was loved by many."

"It must be really cool being from Mumbai. I work with a few people from India. You'll have to tell me all about Mumbai so that I can go back to work and brag that I know something about India that I didn't learn from them."

"Sure. Terrance, we should leave now to make it to the restaurant in time for our reservation."

Charlene was beautiful and relaxed at dinner. Priyanka, on the other hand barely moved her head to be sure she was sitting properly and looking her best. Charlene was not slouching in her chair, but she looked far more relaxed than Priyanka. Priyanka thought Charlene was going to be intimidated by her beauty, but because Charlene was relaxed and talkative, she came across more confident than Priyanka.

"Charlene, Terrance tells me you are a salesperson?"

"Actually, I'm a District Manager, but because I'm so close to my customers, I guess I could be considered a salesperson. I like to think of myself as a hybrid, although my job title is District Manger."

"Charlene's being modest," Terrance interjected after taking time to swallow his food.

"Sounds interesting, but I'm not sure if I would have the patience to deal with clients or customers on that level. I'm sorry do you refer to them as clients or customers?"

"I enjoy my job. I have many clients, and because they are professional, it does not take a lot of patience. It does, however, require me to have a lot of knowledge about their needs and the products we have to meet those needs."

"What is it that you sell?" Priyanka asked sarcastically.

"I sell software. I'm working on a client's project here in New York which is why I'm here but that project will end soon when the client goes live with the software in a couple of months. Now that's enough about me. How did you guys meet?" Charlene asked pointing two fingers in a "V" shape at Priyanka and Terrance.

"Babe, I'll let you tell the story," stated Priyanka.

"We met at the office. Priyanka was the face of the company."

"How so, what do you mean she was the face of the company? Receptionist?"

"I guess you can say that, right babe?" asked Terrance looking at Priyanka for confirmation that he was answering correctly.

"Well, Administrative Assistant, but that's not the case now so finish with your story."

"I see," smiled Charlene as she glanced over at Priyanka and noticed her watching Terrance intently as he told the story of how they met.

"Anyway Charlene, I knew that she was going to be my wife the moment we met. I knew she was checking me out just as much as I was checking her out. The chemistry was there from day one."

"I don't hear any objections from you, Priyanka, so Terrance must be telling the truth."

"I'm embarrassed to say so, but yes. We were like high school kids. We felt the same chemistry but he made the first move. I guess you can say the rest is history."

"You guys are lucky to have found each other, and I can see that you both have equal admiration for each other."

"Thanks, and what about you Charlene. Have you found that special one?" asked Priyanka

"I've come really close but not so lucky in closing the deal. I'm still young and hopeful; I have not given up yet."

"Terrance, your mother must be over joyed."

"Yes, she is. She is very excited to put it mildly. Priyanka and I are going down for a visit next month. Things are moving fast, so we have to make it down there before the wedding."

"Cool. Oh! I almost forgot to mention that I did make that surprise call to Latonja. We must have talked for two hours. She really appreciates what you did for her and her children. She is happy and making an effort to do better. She's even enrolled in a community college studying to be a nurse."

"She's studying to be a nurse at a community college?" asked Priyanka.

"It's possible babe. It may be a two- year program that will allow her to transfer those credits to a University to become a registered nurse."

"I see. I was confused," replied Priyanka

"Priyanka, what about your parents? I'm sure they are as excited as Terrance's parents are about the wedding."

"I wish that were the case, but I have not spoken to my parents since high school. My parents were extremely traditional back then, and I suspect they still are today. They didn't agree with my lack of interest in their traditions. I tried, but I grew to have my own mind. I never fully understood how they expected me to go to school with Americans and not have American friends or embrace the American traditions. Let me stop and not go down that road. Needless to say, it's a sad situation, but I survived on my own. I'm very proud of that. I've accepted the fact that my parents are no longer a part of my life."

"I'm sorry to hear that, Priyanka, but you have done well for yourself, and you're marrying into a great family. I remember feeling so comfortable and at home whenever I had to stay with Terrance and his family. I never admitted that back then because I thought I was grown and old enough to stay home alone. Mrs. Johnson always had a way of making me feel at home. Terrance and I talked about that the last time I was here."

"Oh no, I'm sorry to hear that. Why did you have to stay with Terrance's family? Was your mother on drugs or something?"

Pausing before answering, Charlene took a sip of her wine.

"Quite the opposite, my mother worked during the day and went to school at night, so there were many nights I had to stay with Terrance and his family."

"I'm so sorry. I didn't mean to offend you. It's just that Terrance has told me so many tragic stories about the people he grew up with and the neighborhood. Your mother sounds like she was a wonderful person. Terrance told me that she passed. I'm sorry for your loss."

"She was an amazing mother. Can you guys excuse me for a moment? I need to run to the ladies' room," replied Charlene as she wiped a small tear from her eye.

Terrance didn't notice that Charlene excused herself because she had gotten emotional.

"Do you see what I mean baby? Charlene is cool, right? Did you notice she didn't question you any about your parents?"

"Yes, that was kind of her, and she does seem like a cool person. She's a welcomed difference from Jaylan and Melody, but why didn't you mention she spent so much time with you and your family? You are obviously closer to her than you led me to believe."

"Yes, she did when we were kids. Like I said, she and her mother moved away before we were in high school. We all lost contact with Charlene."

"And you didn't know that her mother had passed?"

"Baby where is all of this coming from? You're starting to worry me. Are you implying something? If you are, you are way off."

"Nothing Baby, I was just asking. Listen, I need to run to the ladies' room myself." Priyanka stood up from the table and kissed Terrance on the cheek before walking away.

Charlene was washing her hands when Priyanka appeared standing at one of the sinks next to her.

"Charlene, I hope you are ok. I didn't mean to make you upset by asking about your mother."

"I'm fine. I get this way sometimes when I talk about my mother, but I do enjoy moments when I can reflect on the time I shared with my mother."

"Good. I'm glad to hear that. I was hoping to catch up with you in here to have a moment away from Terrance. Tell me about your time with Terrance. I didn't realize that you and Terrance spent so much time together. Are you and Terrance hiding something from me?"

"Are you referring to when we were children? You have to be joking with me, right? I have not seen or heard from Terrance since then," replied Charlene with a puzzling, amused and slightly annoyed expression.

"I'm just saying that I didn't know how close you were to Terrance."

"To be honest with you Priyanka, we all were very close when we were children. Terrance, Pookie, Troy, Latonja and I were all like sisters and brothers. I'm sorry you feel there was something more but trust me when I say there was not. Quite honestly, you are barking up the wrong tree."

"You mean as close as Latonja and the guy that died? Pookie, right? Didn't they have children?" asked Priyanka sarcastically.

"Listen girl, I'm not sure what you are looking for, but you have a good man in Terrance. If I were you, I would keep my focus there and not worry about things that don't and have never existed."

"I don't mean to come across as rude, but like you said Terrance is a good man. I can't allow someone off the streets to just walk into our lives and not ask questions."

"Off the streets, are you implying I'm off the streets? Now that's rude, and I'm going to walk away before things get ugly."

"Listen, Charlene, I didn't mean to offend you, and I'm sorry if I have. Can we forget this conversation ever happened? I can see from your reaction that I don't have anything to worry about with you when it comes to Terrance."

"Forgotten, we should get back to our food."

Terrance stood up as both ladies approached the table. He pulled the chair out for Priyanka to have a seat and then proceeded to pull the chair out for Charlene.

"I thought you both got lost in there somewhere."

"No, we didn't, just talking and almost forgot we were having dinner with you." replied Priyanka jokingly.

"Yes, just girl talk," added Charlene with a forced smile.

"Charlene, I meant to ask you while in the ladies' room if you would be in our wedding?"

Charlene turned to look Priyanka in the eyes to see if she was for real. She thought to herself that Priyanka was one crazy lady and Terrance that didn't have a clue. She then turned to look at Terrance to see his reaction to Priyanka's question.

"Do you mean to be in the wedding as in a bridesmaid?"

"That's exactly what I'm asking. I'm short one bridesmaid and what better person than you? Terrance and I would be honored."

"Gosh, I don't know. My schedule is so tight. When and where is it?"

"Come on Charlene. I'm sure you can make it happen. Do your friend a favor," replied Terrance.

Charlene looked over at Terrance. She could not say no to Terrance, as he looked at her with his big beautiful eyes, deep brown skin, white teeth and a smile that could steal candy from Willy Wonka.

"Terrance, since you put it that way, I'm sure I can make it happen. Priyanka please let me know the details as soon as possible so that I can make arrangements around my work schedule."

"Thank you Charlene! This means so much to us." replied Priyanka as she stood up from the table and walked over to hug Charlene as if she was truly appreciative.

"Terrance, do you think you can have the car service take me back to the hotel?"

"We can take you back to the hotel," replied Terrance.

"Terrance, the car service is fine, I don't want you to go out of your way. You guys can go on. I'll hang around here at the bar until the car service is here. I'll be just fine."

"Ok, if you insist, but please call me tomorrow morning before you leave town."

Charlene watched as Terrance and Priyanka walked away. "He has no idea how manipulative that woman is," Charlene thought to herself. She then took a sip of her drink and turned away towards the bar.

CHAPTER 14

Reflections From Priyanka

I

S tanding in the shower with tears running from her eyes as fast as the running water, Priyanka spoke out to herself as if she expected a voice to speak back to her. Holding her head back with the water running down in her face, she yelled out, "Why does this keep happening to me? What did I do to deserve such unrest in my life! I know Charlene is going to tell Terrance about my conversation with her. I just know it! Why didn't I keep my mouth shut? I wasn't expecting her to be so beautiful. I know she's going to come between Terrance and me. I have to find a way to stop her. I don't want to lose Terrance like I lost John. I don't want to have to do to Terrance what I had to do to John."

Priyanka continued talking to herself while falling to the floor of the shower as if she had lost control of the muscles in her legs. She sat in the corner of the shower pulling and holding her knees towards her chest with the water still running. "John, you made me do it! You made me hurt you! All I wanted was for you to love me. I would have been yours forever. Why did you have to dig into my past?" After speaking to John for several minutes as if he was there with her, she stood up and reached for the water handle to turn off the water.

She dried her face and wiped the tears from her eyes and continued talking to herself. "I have to stay calm and do things differently. I have to stop these running thoughts in my head but, I will not let Charlene come between Terrance and me. I don't want her in my wedding, but I have to know what she is doing when it comes to Terrance at all times. Oh, my God! Why does this keep happening to me? Why did Jaylan have to see me with that fool Grant? I know Grant wants me to admit that I'm that girl from high school that he used and left for his girlfriend, but I won't. All he wants to do is to play hero and run to Mark and my family. Why can't these people move on and leave me alone?

I left Wisconsin as poor little Natalie with my son Justin years ago for a reason." Priyanka stepped out of the shower, put on her robe and walked to the mirror. "I'm Priyanka now, and no one can change that. I mean no one." She smiled and walked away from the mirror.

CHAPTER 15

Priyanka Goes To Alabama

One month after running into Charlene in New York, Terrance booked a flight for him and Priyanka to visit with his family in Alabama. Priyanka felt it was a good time to finally meet Terrance's family face-to-face. She was a little nervous at first about meeting his family because she thought Charlene was sure to tell Terrance and his family all about her conversation in the ladies' room the first night she met Charlene. Terrance had not said anything, so she felt confident that Charlene had kept it between the two of them as she had promised.

Terrance and Priyanka had dinner with Jaylan and Melody several times before leaving for Alabama. Terrance wanted Jaylan, Melody and Priyanka all to feel comfortable around each other. Each time Melody had to remind Jaylan to keep his questions to himself when it concerned anything about Priyanka's past. She especially warned him never to mention anything about the strange man pulling on Priyanka's arm since Terrance had accepted her explanation.

A few nights before his flight, Terrance called his parents to remind them not to ask Priyanka about her past. He asked his mother to mention it to other family members that may be around when he and Priyanka arrived in town.

"I guess I understand how she feels being abandoned by her family, but you make it seem so serious. I'm almost afraid to talk to her without a script in front of me. I'm just not used to carefully selecting words when talking to people. I don't want to say anything or want anyone else to say anything to offend her. We all want her to feel right at home, so we will let her lead the conversations and take it from there. How does that sound?"

"Thank you, mom. All you all have to do is to open your hearts to her. She's an amazing person."

Terrance was not aware that his mother had planned a family reunion with extended family members and friends to celebrate his engagement. She also invited Latonja and to add to the surprise she invited Jaylan, Melody and Charlene.

The flight was scheduled to arrive at 2:00 p.m. on Saturday afternoon. Mrs. Johnson, Terrance's mother, arranged for everyone to meet at her home at 1:00 p.m. She wanted to make sure that the meat was on the grill cooking and that everyone was in place when Terrance and Priyanka arrived.

Jaylan, Melody and Charlene all arrived Friday night. Jaylan and Melody were staying at the same hotel as Charlene so they arranged to have dinner with Charlene to get to know her because they had not had the opportunity to meet her in person. They had only heard good things about her from Terrance.

Jaylan saw a woman standing at the front of the entrance to the restaurant looking as though she was lost.

"Excuse me, are you Charlene?"

Looking up from her purse, Charlene replied. "Yes. And you must be Jaylan?"

"Yes, nice to meet you. Jaylan extended his hand for a handshake. "We are sitting over there." Jaylan led her to the table where Melody was seated.

"This is my wife Melody," he said as they reached the table.

Melody greeted her with a handshake and a smile.

Barely seated, Charlene immediately started talking.

"I'm so glad you guys called me to have dinner. It's nice to finally meet the two of you. I've heard so much about you that I feel confident in saying that your marriage is Terrance's inspiration."

"Thank you for meeting us and we've heard a lot of nice things about you as well," replied Melody.

"Terrance is almost a married man. I'm so happy for him. He has always been determined. Even as a kid he would talk about how he was going to make it so that he could take care of his family."

"Yes girl, that's Terrance, and according to my husband Jay, it didn't take long for him to fall in love with Priyanka." Melody, looking over at Jaylan, raised her hand to get the attention of the server to let him know they were ready to order.

"He did tell me he knew she was the one for him the moment he laid eyes on her. She seems like an intelligent girl, and she's beautiful," remarked Charlene looking closely at the expressions on both Jaylan's and Melody's faces to see if there was a reaction as to how they truly felt about Priyanka.

"Terrance is the man," Jaylan replied sarcastically.

"Jay, don't start with that. Charlene, as you can probably feel, my husband believes that Terrance is moving too fast. He's not too happy about this marriage. He wants Terrance to slow down to get to know Priyanka better. Me, I see no reason to wait if he feels she's the one. He adores Priyanka."

"It's been a year, right?" asked Charlene.

"It will be by the time they are married. It's not that I want him to wait just for the hell of it. He knows very little about her, and there's something about her that I don't trust. I don't think she's the person she is pretending to be. But with all that being said, I still support my man in his decision."

Pausing for a moment to order their food, Charlene wondered if she should mention the conversation she had with Priyanka about Terrance.

"To be honest with you Melody, I kind of agree with Jaylan. I have not known Priyanka as long as you guys have, but the limited contact I've had with her has been less than pleasant. First, before I say anything, please promise that you guys won't say anything to Terrance. I would hate to hurt his feelings. He is such an honest and nice guy."

"Trust me, we won't say a word," promised Melody, speaking before Jaylan could open his mouth.

"Gosh, I don't know how to say this, but she cornered me in the ladies'room when I met her and Terrance for dinner to get to know her. She followed me to the ladies' room, and she basically accused me of having romantic feelings for Terrance and trying to take him away from her."

"Shut up. You got to be kidding me!"

"I'm not sure what she was implying, but it was not a good look for her. I mean she is a beautiful girl with a man who adores her. You would think that was enough. To make matters even stranger, she asked me to be in their wedding after accusing me of trying to take her man. Who does that?"

Jaylan, taking it all in allowed Melody to do all the responding.

"What did you say?"

"I agreed to be in the wedding but only because of Terrance. She asked me in front of him. I couldn't say no. Another weird thing is that Terrance says it makes her sad to talk about her parents."

"Yeah, that's my husband's problem with her."

"Jaylan, I think your concerns are valid. My mother passed away suddenly, and I'm sad about that, I can't pretend nor do I want to pretend that she did not exist. Her parents are still living, right?"

"Charlene, you're my kind of people! That's exactly what I have been trying to get my wife to see. There is something not right with that girl."

"I hear you both, but we have to trust that Terrance knows what he is doing. Maybe Priyanka will chill out once she is married. Maybe she's just trying too hard to impress us. I think all she wants is to fit in with his family and friends."

"Maybe and you are right. We have to support Terrance no matter the situation," Charlene replied.

"Absolutely, we are here as a surprise to Terrance, so we have to be on our best behavior. We have to be open to Priyanka and make her feel that we accept her into our lives and trust that she will be there for Terrance. Now let's drink to a happy life for Terrance and Priyanka," Melody suggested, while holding her glass up high to toast for a happy life for their friend Terrance.

Mr. Johnson, Terrance's father, was asked to pick Terrance and Priyanka up from the airport. He stood at the gate waiting while silently practicing what he would say to Priyanka. He was not around when his wife spoke to Priyanka over the phone, so he didn't know what to expect. Being a good listener made him a man of few words. He was not a talker at all. People would joke that conversations with him were awkward. He listened and smiled and every now and then he would add a word or two to the conversation. Whenever his advice was solicited he would always advise, "You have to do what's best for you because only you have to live with whatever you are dealing with," no matter what he was asked.

Terrance and Priyanka had been at the gate waiting for Mr. Johnson for nearly thirty minutes before Terrance decided to call his mother to see if his father was in route to the airport. In the meantime, Mr. Johnson was still standing eagerly at the wrong gate waiting. He didn't bother to look at the paper his wife had given him with all the information written down. He simply stopped at the first gate where he saw others waiting.

Mrs. Johnson informed Terrance that his father should have been at the airport by now because he left the house in plenty of time to be there for his arrival. She told Terrance to look around because she believed his father was waiting in the wrong place. Terrance told Priyanka to wait at the baggage claim and that he was going to look for his father. Priyanka rolled her eyes and wondered how one could get lost in such a small airport. It was not even half as big as the airport in Atlanta. Terrance pretended not to see the frustrated look on Priyanka's face. He was frustrated, too but appreciative that his father had taken the time to come to the airport to pick them up.

Terrance finally saw his father standing at a gate where a flight from Chicago was to arrive. He walked over to his father. He was surprised to see Terrance standing there.

"Thanks Dad for picking us up," stated Terrance while giving his dad a hug.

"Where did you come from? I didn't see you go by?"

"We were at another gate. We've been here for about thirty minutes. I'm sorry for the confusion. Mom probably didn't give you the flight number, so you could see it over there." Terrance pointing at the display above them with the gate information based on flight number.

"Oh, I would have never thought to look above, and your mama did give me a piece of paper. I just didn't bother to look at it."

"No problem, next time just ask someone at the desk. They will be able to tell you exactly where to go because the display can even be confusing."

"Where's Peria?" asked Mr. Johnson.

"Dad, her name is Priyanka, and she is waiting for us at baggage claim."

"Ok, let's go get her. We have to be getting on back to the house."

Mr. Johnson, slightly hunched over, turned to follow Terrance.

"Dad, this is my beautiful future wife, Priyanka."

Priyanka turned around to see Terrance standing there with his father.

"Hello young lady. You sure are beautiful. I don't know if my son deserves such a fine looking young lady as you."

"Thank you Mr. Johnson, you are so kind, and it's a pleasure to meet you."

"I'm sorry I kept y'all waiting, but they make things so complicated these days."

Mr. Johnson smiled at Priyanka, picked up a couple of bags and led the way to the car without saying another word.

Priyanka thought it was strange that Mr. Johnson was such a quiet man. Terrance had already informed her that his father was a man of few words.

Terrance sat in the front seat on the passenger side while his father drove ten miles below the speed limit. The ride to the house was quiet and long. Every so often Priyanka would ask a question to try to make conversation with Mr. Johnson. Terrance would wait a few seconds to see if his father would respond. When he didn't, Terrance would end up carrying the conversation. The conversation went on this way the entire ride. Although Priyanka thought Mr. Johnson was awkward, she liked him and felt a sense of calmness around him because he didn't talk a lot, and he didn't ask questions.

Everyone had gathered in the backyard as Mrs. Johnson had planned. The back yard was filled with smoke from the barbecue grill. Mrs. Johnson was swiftly moving from the backyard to the kitchen making sure everything was in order before Terrance and Priyanka arrived. She instructed everyone to park alongside the street and not in the driveway because she didn't want to let on to Terrance that there were a lot of people there to celebrate his engagement. She had her grandson standing guard in the front room to alert her when his grandfather arrived with Terrance and Priyanka.

Priyanka stared out the window looking at all the houses in the neighborhood. She was surprised to see that the neighborhood was not as she had thought it would be. She had never been to the south, so her image of the south was an image of dirt roads and pick-up trucks She saw none of this. She saw nice, modest homes and well-kept yards. As they approached his parents' home, Terrance could see there were an unusual number of cars parked along the street.

"Someone must be having a party or something," he stated.

"I was thinking the same thing," replied Priyanka looking over at Mr. Johnson.

"I don't get in other folks' business, so I don't know if they are or not," replied Mr. Johnson.

When he saw them pull into the driveway, Terrance's nephew ran to the backyard to let everyone know that his grandfather had arrived with Terrance and Priyanka,

Terrance and Priyanka entered the house with Mr. Johnson following. He told Terrance that his mother was in the backyard cooking on the grill.

Priyanka stopped to look at all the pictures surrounding the room. She was used to seeing paintings, sculptures or other forms of art on the walls, but the walls were filled with pictures of Terrance and his family. It was almost as if she had walked into a history museum featuring only Terrance's family. There were black and white pictures of Terrance's grandparents and great grandparents. There were pictures of Terrance's parents before marriage, after marriage, before children and after children. There were pictures of Terrance and his siblings and pictures of his siblings with their families. Then there was Terrance in a present-day picture, standing alone in. Priyanka wondered why Mrs. Johnson had not put up any of the pictures of her and Terrance because she knew that Terrance had sent her many.

Mr. Johnson turned off into another room as Terrance and Priyanka finally entered part of the kitchen leading to the back porch. Before Terrance and Priyanka could reach the first step out the door, everyone yelled, "Congratulations!"

Terrance was overjoyed. He made his way through the crowd of family and friends while introducing Priyanka. He was surprised to see Jaylan, Melody, Charlene and Latonja all standing with their arms crossed waiting for him to notice they were there.

"Get out of here! You guys are no good! You all knew about this all along!"

"Yes, yes, yes, your mother swore us to secrecy," replied Melody.

"This is so cool! Right, Baby?" Terrance questioned looking at Priyanka.

"Yes Baby, I knew something was up when I saw all the cars outside," revealed Priyanka as she hugged each of them and stopping, as she approached an unfamiliar face.

"And you are?" asked Priyanka as she made her way to Latonja.

"Baby, this is the one and only Latonja."

"And you know it! Ms. L's in the house!" shouted Latonja as she greeted both Terrance and Priyanka in her loud and funny way.

"It's nice to finally meet you. Terrance told me all about you when he was up here the last time with his home folks."

Smiling as much as she could to avoid showing what she was feeling, Priyanka continued to smile as Latonja continued to speak.

"I hear you from India or somewhere in the Middle East. How far is that from here?"

"I haven't really thought about it. Do you know, Baby?" Priyanka asked looking for Terrance to rescue her from Latonja.

"Baby, that's Latonja for you. She's full of questions."

Charlene stood watching without commenting. She was enjoying the moment. She could see that Priyanka was uncomfortable talking to Latonja.

"You real cute though, but you don't look like no Indian to me. You look like a cute black girl, so you real lucky being from India and looking the way you do. I expected to see you dressed in a lot of clothes with only your eyes showing or a red dot or something in the middle of your head."

At this point, Priyanka felt the only way to get rid of Latonja was to talk back to her as politely as she could.

"No, I don't wear a dot on my head. I was born in Mumbai, India. I'm sure you have no clue where that is, but I was actually raised in New York. The last I remembered the dot is not part of New York's culture. I assume you are from around here, right?"

Latonja walked closer to Priyanka facing her eye to eye.

"Terrance, you got yourself a real smarty pants here, but to answer your question, I'm not from around here. I'm from the other side, but thanks to Terrance, me and my boys live close to here. And why you don't have no foreign accent?"

"Latonja, let's go eat some of this good food that Mrs. Johnson has prepared for everyone," Interrupted Charlene as Terrance motioned to her to rescue Priyanka from Latonja's colorful personality.

"She got a real funky attitude, right? I know she cute, but what does Terrance see in her. She acts like she better than me. I knew she was uppity as soon as I saw her. If Terrance can go away and make all that money and come back and treat people like he got some sense, then anybody can. I can see now that I won't be staying here too long today because I'll have Terrance divorced before he even married," stated Latonja as she was led away by Charlene.

"She's not that bad, Latonja. She's just not used to people coming at her the way you did. I know you meant well, but she just has a different personality. She does not know you the way we do, so try to be nice to her if only for Terrance."

"I guess you right. I'm just going to stay out of her way."

"That was strange," stated Priyanka to Terrance referring to Latonja.

"That's Latonja's personality, Baby, so don't take it personally. She didn't mean any disrespect. It was her way of trying to get to know you. She will be ok, so don't stress over it."

"If you say so," replied Priyanka looking at Jaylan and Melody with a smile as if she didn't believe Terrance.

"Thanks again guys for coming all this way for the surprise; we need to make our way over to mom. I know she is wondering what's taking us so long. I can see it in her eyes from here."

Priyanka took a deep breath as she approached Mrs. Johnson. She didn't know what to expect after meeting Latonja.

"Goodness, you are even more beautiful in person than you are on all those pictures Terrance sent to us. Give me a hug."

"It's so nice to finally meet you too, Mrs. Johnson."

"Did y'all have a good flight?"

"Yes, we did have a good flight, and thank you so much for the surprise. I've waited so long to meet you that I need to pinch myself now that I'm here face-to-face with you. It was sweet of Mr. Johnson to pick us up from the airport, too"

"Better late than never and how else was y'all going to make it from the airport? I know y'all tired from the plane ride. Go on upstairs to freshen up and put y'all stuff up. Come on back down when y'all are done. Terrance, you staying in the first room on the right and Priyanka, I fixed the room up next to me and my husband for you. It's the second door on the left."

"Oh no, Mrs. Johnson, I would never impose on you and Mr. Johnson. I made reservations at the hotel for Terrance and me, so we are fine."

"Then how am I supposed to get to know you if you at the hotel?"

"Baby, Mom is right. We should stay here. I didn't know you made reservations at the hotel. I had planned on us staying here since we will only be here for a couple of days."

"Baby, I'm sorry. I didn't know your plans," replied Priyanka.

"Don't worry. Now, y'all go on up and freshen up."

Priyanka was not happy with staying at the house. She felt that Terrance should have agreed with her and not put her on the spot, but she didn't say anything to Terrance. Her mission was to meet everyone and to get them all to like her. She knew that nothing more than her getting along with his family would make Terrance happier.

As she and Terrance walked down the hallway leading to the room where she was staying, she saw Mr. Johnson sitting in a chair watching TV. Mr. Johnson looked up as he heard noise next to his room. He looked at Priyanka, waved, smiled, and then went back to watching his TV. She started to ask him why he was in the room watching TV when there was a party going on in the back yard. She decided not to ask because she knew he would not have a reply, and that would present an awkward quietness. She smiled back instead and continued on to the room she had been assigned.

Priyanka managed to make it through the party with no more awkward moments between her and Latonja. Charlene told Latonja what she knew about Priyanka's situation with her family. If anyone understood growing up in a dysfunctional family, it was Latonja. By the end of the party, Priyanka felt love and respect from everyone in attendance. Even the children loved her.

CHAPTER 16

Priyanka's Reflections

II

"Terrance's family was not as bad as I had made them out to be in my head. His father is strange, but I can live with his uniqueness. I have not quite figured out his mother, but she seems nice enough. Latonja was just as I had perceived her to be based on what Terrance had told me about her. I'm not worried about her. I doubt if I will ever see her again. One thing that I did notice about her was that she is very perceptive. She is the only person that I am aware, outside of the people from my past, who suspects that I'm black. She may not have verbalized it, but I could tell she did not believe me when I told her that I was from Mumbai, India. At any rate, she's not someone that I would lose sleep over. She's too simple. Grant, on the other hand, worries me. He is determined to get me to confess to being someone that I'm not. I'm not Natalie anymore. I don't even remember that girl. If it had not been for the wedding planner, I would have never crossed path with him. I knew I should not have gone back up there the next day, but I had to try to convince him that I was not the person he thought I was. Needless to say, he didn't buy it. He went on and on and would not accept that I was not that person. That's when I decided to leave, but he would not release my arm. That's when Jaylan happened to see me struggling with him. Little did I know that Jaylan would be there that day. Later that same day, when the dust settled, I was able to locate where Grant works and where he lives. Now, I must make contact with him again to fix this problem. Seeing him that day only brought back memories of me being that stupid girl who thought that I could have him just because of my looks. I've grown to know that looks are only half the battle in this world. Why was he insisting on talking to me anyway? Was he trying to hit on me, or was he simply trying to get information for Mark and his family or my family, for that matter. Whatever the case may be, I'm not that girl anymore, and I'm never going to be that girl again. I have a new life with a wonderful man and a great future ahead. No one is going to interfere with that.

CHAPTER 17

Jaylan

Jaylan left Alabama with more questions about Priyanka. He was happy to see that Priyanka was polite to Terrance's family and that they all got along well and seemed to really like Priyanka. In all the time that Jaylan had known Terrance, he had never seen Terrance as happy as he was the day he introduced Priyanka to him family. For that reason alone, Jaylan went back and forth with his doubts. "Maybe Priyanka is who she says she is and is really hurt by her past. On the other hand, there might besomething in her past that's she hiding and if so, how could it affect Terrance?" He understood her shortness with Latonja, but he thought her response was condescending. Worse, it seemed to have come naturally. But what bothered Jaylan the most was the stranger that Priyanka said she didn't know. He wished that he had gotten more information from the guy and not have allowed Priyanka to rush him away. After thinking about it more, he felt that Priyanka knew the stranger. He then thought about the box that Priyanka had hidden in her closet. Jaylan knew that he would not be at rest with the marriage until he had at least seen the contents in that box. He thought of no way to view the contents of that box other than to break into Terrance's apartment while Terrance and Priyanka were at work. He wanted to tell his wife of his plans but decided against it because he knew she would talk him out of it. Jaylan had planned to break into the apartment on a Wednesday because Wednesday was the longest working day of the week for both Terrance and Priyanka.

CHAPTER 18

Priyanka Calls In Sick

It was Wednesday; Priyanka knew this was the day she had to make her move with Grant. She knew that Terrance would be working in the office late as they both did each Wednesday. Therefore, she called the office to let them know that she would not be in because she was not feeling well. She told Terrance that she was going to sleep in all day. She was able to contact Grant and had asked if he would meet her for a late lunch. Grant agreed and thanked her for contacting him because he was sure she was Natalie without a doubt. Priyanka told him there was a reason why she was hiding and would explain everything to him when they met for lunch. Grant decided he would wait before he spoke to anyone about meeting up with Natalie. Most people in her hometown had assumed she was dead and had stopped talking about her disappearance. But there was one person who Grant knew cared, and he wanted nothing more than to be the person to tell Mark that he had found Natalie and his son Justin. He knew that Mark never gave up on finding his son Justin.

"Thank you for meeting me on such short notice," greeted Priyanka as she sat down at the table where Grant was waiting to meet her.

"No problem. How did you find me? I've been racking my brain trying to figure that out."

"Let's just say it was not difficult and leave it at that," replied Priyanka with a smile."

"I took the rest of the day off since it's past lunch time, and we have a lot of catching up to do. I will say that you have taken care of yourself."

Licking her lips and leaning towards Grant, Priyanka smiled.

"Thank you, and you are not so bad yourself. So, tell me did you end up marrying Meredith?"

"No, that was a high school thing. Once we left for college our relationship turned to more of a friendship. She's married to a doctor and living quite well. She worked as an attorney before her children. She lives in Atlanta. My wife and I are friends with her and her husband. Last year, we took our kids on a cruise with Meredith and her family."

"You have children?" asked Priyanka.

"Of course, I do. Does that surprise you?"

"No. Not at all."

"What have you been doing with yourself, Natalie? Why did you leave town without telling anyone? Most people back home believed that you and your son were kidnapped and killed. You guys were in the news for weeks. Your poor mom was on TV pleading for your return, and Mark, I won't even go into his pleading. It's been nearly fifteen years now, right?"

"Yes, it has been fifteen years. Gosh, where do I start? I won't make excuses, but I had to leave. First my family abused me. My father was constantly upset over something. No one outside of my family knew it, but there were times when my father would beat me for weeks for no reason at all. My mother did nothing about it. I moved in with Mark's family after I got pregnant because I didn't want to bring my child into an abusive home. Later, after the baby was born, I overheard Mark's mother speaking to someone over the phone making arrangements to have my baby adopted by someone in another country. They were more concerned about Mark and his football career than they were about my baby and me. I decided that we had to leave. I didn't know what else to do. I've left that life behind me. Grant, I'm here today to beg you to please let my son and I live in peace. He's 15 now and a good child. He knows nothing of what I left behind. We have a good life. Please don't mess up things for my son. What I did was wrong, but please believe me when I say I had no other choice."

"I can't believe that Mark would have allowed his son to be sent to another country. All he used to talk about was providing a good future for you and his son. I even doubt if Mark's mother would do something like that. They took you in and cared for you when they didn't have to. I know these people. They would never do something as low as to plan to have your baby sent to another country without your knowledge. It's just not adding up. Now tell me why you really left?"

"Grant, you would never understand. You come from a different world. You knew nothing of the problems I dealt with when I was living at home with my family and with Mark and his family. Mark's father even made a pass at me. I was afraid that something bad might happen to me when no one was home. I never said anything about that to anyone. It was too much so I had to leave."

"Why do you think I would not understand? Are you saying that because I'm a white guy?"

"No, because you come from a rich family."

"What does that have to do with me trying to understand why you left the way you did. For a while, to be honest, I thought your son was my baby, and you left because you could not handle living a lie. I guess I was wrong there."

"Mark never knew about us, and we had a paternity test done. Justin is Mark's son without a doubt, and besides you stopped seeing me. I was not good enough for you, remember?"

"Natalie, I stopped seeing you because I was involved with Meredith, and you knew it. It was as if you were trying to get to Meredith through me. You wanted to hurt her for some reason. You only wanted me because I was with her."

"Please call me Priyanka. I'm Priyanka. Can we take this conversation somewhere private? Like is there a hotel or something around here? I just want you to understand where I'm coming from. And I know what you want by the way you are looking at me. Remember those high school days in the closet?"

"Since you put it like that I'll call you whatever you want me to, and I do know of a place. My place. I have a condo here in town for those nights I'm too tired to drive home."

"You mean you have a place out here? Does your wife know about this place?"

"Let's not bring my wife into this. Are we leaving now or what?" asked Grant as he motioned the waiter for their tab. "And for the record, she does know about my condo. It was actually her idea to keep me from driving home whenever I'm working late."

"I see you have not changed much; once a cheater always a cheater."

"Natalie, I mean Priyanka, I've always had a weakness for you. I can't believe it still exists after all these years."

Priyanka and Grant arrived at his condo. She was careful to watch for cameras in the hallway and she allowed Grant to hold the door open for her because she didn't want to touch anything. She didn't want any traces of her ever being at the condo. Grant told her to have a seat while he went to freshen up. He told Priyanka to make herself comfortable as he handed her two wine glasses and pointed to where the wine was located. Everything was going as she had planned. She knew that Grant would not be able to resist her and would accept her invitation to go somewhere private. Grant's having a condo in town made her plan that much better.

"Priyanka, I'm glad you're here, and I'm sorry to hear about all you went through with your family and Mark's family. Mark was so in love with you that I can't imagine he would have allowed his family to mistreat you, but I wasn't there so who am I to say whether or not you are telling the truth."

"Grant, Mark's family did not necessarily treat me bad. They were sneaky and were planning to give my baby away, so I had no choice but to leave. I never knew if his father would one day attack me when no one was around. They only cared about Mark, and why are we going over this again? I thought you wanted me here for something else." Priyanka sat next to Grant on the sofa and leaned forward to undo his shirt.

"Speaking of your son, where is he?"

Priyanka immediately moved her hand away from Grant's chest, looked him in his eyes with contempt, and rapidly stood up from the sofa and picked up her purse.

"Why you are so interested is a better question! I'm leaving; I should have never come here anyway." Priyanka reached in her purse as if she was trying to feel for her keys.

"Natalie, you are lying about something! Where is your son? What the hell have you done with that child?"

Pulling a small handgun from her purse, she pointed it at his chest and fired three shots. "None of your damn business!"

Priyanka remained calm. She carefully put the two wine glasses in her bag and removed Grant's shirt. She rolled the gun up into the shirt and placed it in her bag with the two glasses. She stood there looking at the body for a few seconds to be sure that Grant was not moving. She didn't touch the body because she was sure he was dead. Once she felt it was safe to leave, she opened the door with a paper towel wrapped around the knob, put on a cap to cover her face and walked down the empty hallway as if she had not just shot a man. She kept her head down to avoid what she thought were cameras. She did not see anyone around as she exited the building.

Once in the car, Priyanka wiped her fingers prints from the gun, ripped Grant's shirt into strips of pieces and drove by a nearby river and threw the gun out of the window. She threw the glasses out the window on the highway, shattering them into pieces and threw strips of the shirt out of the window from the highway to several different streets far away from her home. By the time she reached home, she was relaxed and relived that Grant was no longer a threat to her happiness.

Later on, that night, as Terrance was in the shower, Priyanka turned on the TV to watch the news to see if there was anything on there about Grant. She wanted to confirm that he was found dead.

"Since when have you been interested in the local news?" asked Terrance as he entered the room to find Priyanka watching.

"I was just turning the channels and stopped here for some reason."

"You should find something less depressing to watch. The news is always full of stories of crime."

Priyanka changed the channel as Terrance had requested. She decided that it was best that she read it in the newspaper or on the internet the following morning.

The next morning Priyanka found out that Grant was not dead and that he was in the hospital in critical condition. The doctors were not expecting him to live and had placed him in a medically induced coma.

Grant's wife was the reason he was found in time. She was expecting Grant to call her after work, but after several hours passed and she had not heard from him she became concerned. She then called the front office of their condo and asked security to check to see if Grant was in their apartment. It was unlike Grant not to be in touch with her.

The security guy knocked once and the door opened. He proceeded to push the door open further. There he saw Grant lying face down on the floor shirtless in a pool of blood. He checked to see if Grant was breathing.

Grant was barely breathing. He called 911 and then the front desk to let them know that Grant had been shot.

Later that night, the word had spread. It was all over the news. People were shocked. The building was in a prominent area where violent crimes didn't take place. The police department provided a number for people to call with any information that may lead to finding the person who had committed the crime. The police suspected that Grant must have known the person and had invited the person into his condo because there was no evidence of a break-in.

Priyanka didn't panic because as she thought more about it and what Grant knew about her, she realized that Grant knew nothing about her other than her first name.

She assumed Grant had told no one back in their home state of their meeting because she had not confessed anything to him. She knew Grant would wait until he had evidence that she was Natalie.

What she didn't know was that Grant had been in contact with Mark. He told Mark he was not sure but he felt confident that he had found Natalie. He told Mark he would be back in contact with him once he had more information.

A couple of weeks had passed since the shooting. Priyanka secretly kept up with what was going on with Grant by reading information on the internet. Grant was still alive, but he was no longer in local headline news.

CHAPTER 19

Terrance

Terrance was happier than he had been in his whole life. He finally felt like he was becoming the man he had always dreamed of becoming. He had a career that was on a top executive track and he was soon to be married to the woman he had always hoped for. He was happy that Jaylan had finally accepted Priyanka and, more importantly, his family adored her. Terrance didn't think it could get any better until one day when he was called into his boss's office and was informed that he had been promoted. The promotion came with a bigger officer and a higher salary.

Terrance immediately called his mother to give her the good news about his promotion. He enjoyed giving his mother news about his accomplishments. He knew it was like hearing her favorite music when either of her children were doing well and were happy.

Later that day, Terrance told Priyanka about his promotion. She was almost as excited as Terrance. She told Terrance she knew he was the man God had for her the moment she met him. Priyanka was truly proud of the man she was about to call her husband.

Terrance decided he wanted to celebrate by inviting his closest friends to his apartment for dinner. Priyanka told him it was a great idea, but deep down she was not happy. She wanted a celebration with Terrance alone. She still did not trust Jaylan or Charlene. Although Charlene had not given Priyanka any indication that she had doubts about her, Priyanka still felt she could not trust Charlene, and she knew that Jaylan had not changed his opinion of her.

Priyanka then thought that maybe the celebration would afford her one last opportunity to make a good impression. She agreed with Terrance and made the calls to Jaylan and Charlene inviting them to dinner.

Everyone arrived as planned and greeted Priyanka as she answered the door while Terrance sat on the deck grilling.

With limited space on the deck, Jaylan managed to sneak up behind Terrance and tackled him as if they were on a football field.

"You the man!" replied Jaylan as he tackled Terrance.

Terrance thanked Jaylan for coming after they settled down.

"Congratulations Terrance! I knew it would not take you long to move up the ladder. I told Jaylan that during your first month at the firm," stated Melody.

"I see why this man married you," replied Terrance as he greeted her with a hug.

"And Charlene, what can I say? You didn't have to come all this way, but your presence is always appreciated," commented Terrance as he gave her a hug.

"Yes, Terrance, we all are very proud of you. Let's all toast to Terrance," stated Priyanka as she poured champagne into five champagne glasses.

Everyone held their glasses high and toasted Terrance's continued success.

"Priyanka, everything looks so nice," stated Melody.

"Thanks. You know me, anything to please my husband. He wanted to share this moment with the special people in his life."

"So, we are done with all the fittings and rehearsals, right Priyanka?" asked Jaylan.

"We are almost there Jaylan. There's only a month left before the wedding. You should see how lovely your wife looks in her dress."

"Ah, thank you Priyanka. You are so kind," replied Melody.

"Priyanka, I must say Terrance is going to pass out after he sees you in that beautiful wedding dress you have," Charlene interjected.

"Thank you Charlene. I was about to say you were very quiet today. Did you just get into town?"

"No, I've been here for a few days now."

"Oh, Terrance and I thought you came just for this occasion."

"I was wondering why Terrance made that statement earlier. I love Terrance, but not enough to make a special trip just to celebrate his promotion," Charlene jokingly replied.

Everyone laughed, but Priyanka didn't appreciate the comment. She slammed her glass on the table and faced Charlene with a frown on her face.

"Well, at least now he knows you love him! We don't have to wonder anymore. You've said it out loud!"

Uncertain, Charlene didn't know what to think of Priyanka's reaction.

"Wait, are you being serious?" Clearly you don't think I mean *love* in a romantic way, right? If by chance you are not joking, then you need to rethink your situation. Terrance and I are just friends, as I have told you before."

Everyone was silent and looked at Priyanka waiting for her reply. Terrance thought Priyanka had put to rest her insecurities about Charlene, and he couldn't ignore what Charlene said to Priyanka. He wondered if Priyanka had made similar accusations before.

"Ladies, ladies, let's not spoil Terrance's moment. I'm sure this is just a misunderstanding. Priyanka you should know by now that Terrance only has eyes for you, so chill and don't let your nerves get the best of you. Terrance, what kind of meat are you cooking over here?" Melody asked, attempting to change the subject and mood.

Holding the fork in his hand while looking over at Priyanka and speaking directly to Charlene.

"Charlene, what do you mean? Has there been such a discussion before, Priyanka?"

"Baby, I have no idea what she is talking about. Of course, not honey. If that were the case, I'm sure Charlene would have told you by now and would not have agreed to be in our wedding. Correct, Charlene?"

"Yes, Priyanka you are correct. I guess I just misunderstood your reaction. And to answer your question Terrance, there were no previous discussions."

CHAPTER 20

Priyanka Reflections

III

"I felt it in my heart the first moment I laid eyes on them that they would be good parents for my little Justin. I saw the love they shared when they looked at each other. There was no way that I could have kept Justin and raised him to have the type of life I had always wanted. It was not the right time for me. Mark and his family did not deserve him after the way they treated me. I knew they were going to put me out of their home, take Justin away from me and raise him to hate me. My little Justin deserved better than Mark and his family. I remember the day as if it was yesterday. I found the most exclusive adoption agency in Maine. It was the best in the country. I took a train to Maine with my baby the morning that I left Mark and his family. I must have watched dozens of couples before I made my decision. Justin was too young to know what was happening to him, and he barely knew me because Mark's mother acted as if he was her child. I made my choice the day that I saw the same couple twice in two weeks. They stepped out of a Mercedes. The husband walked over to the passenger's side of the car and opened the door for his wife. They held hands as if they were truly in love as they walked to the building. I patiently waited with little Justin bundled up to protect him from the cold. It was so cold that I almost left after waiting for an hour, but just as I was in motion to leave, I saw them leaving, each with a smile on their faces. I politely and softly approached the couple and asked if I might speak to them for a moment. His wife looked past me and immediately put her attention on Justin as I held him close to me to protect him from the bitter winds. The husband hesitated but felt his wife's concern and said that they would talk to me, but that we must go inside to get the baby out of the cold. He tried leading me into the adoption agency's building, but I insisted that we go to the building parallel to the adoption agency. Once we were in the building, I removed the covers from Justin's face. The wife could not control herself. She started raving over how beautiful a baby he was. They could see that Justin was well taken care of and was a happy baby by his pumped round face and friendly smile.

I told them that I was from an abusive family and that I could not afford to keep the baby, but I wanted to make the choice of who I gave my baby to. I told them that I had been at the agency looking for several weeks trying to find a home with good people for my baby. Of course, they had questions, but they really wanted a baby, especially the wife. They told me they felt they were going to be approved through the adoption agency, but because of the process, it would be another six months to a year before they would actually know if they were approved. Even then, it would take another six months before they were given a baby. They felt Justin and I being there on that cold day was fate. I felt the same because during the two weeks that I had scoped out the place, they were the only couple that I saw twice.

I told them I wanted them to have my baby after hearing that the father was a general surgeon and the mother was a corporate attorney. They had the means to raise my baby the way that I could not have at the time, and I didn't want him to live a life of struggles while I found my way to success. I believe when a child is born, parents should be ready to give that child a good life, not an average or below average life but a good life. I've never understood the statement, "money does not buy happiness." I've never bought into it, and I firmly believe it's used only by people too lazy to make things happen for themselves. The family invited Justin and me to stay with them for a few days. I asked if we could stay a week so that I could get to know them better. Of course the wife was excited about it, so the husband had no choice but to agree. It was probably the best week of my life at the time. We dined at the finest restaurants. The room where I stayed with Justin was like a presidential suite at a fancy hotel. I told nothing of my family or Mark's family, and I was in Maine several states away from them so there was no way any of their paths would cross. After a week, I knew that I had to say good bye to Justin. It was like he had become so attached to me in the short time that he and I were on our journey to Maine. He never cried for Mark's mother and seemed happy at my very presence. I don't know if he understood or not, but he had a look in his eyes as if he knew that I was about to leave him forever. I never thought that it would affect me emotionally, but his sad eyes touched by heart. I couldn't leave that day as I had planned. I couldn't take the look in his eyes which is why I disappeared a few nights later, in the middle of the night, after everyone was sleeping. I'm not sure how the family handled it, but my suspicion is that they never tried to track me down and they never reported it to anyone. Justin is fifteen today. I never think about him on his birthday as I see in the movies because I know that he has a good life, one that I could not have provided for him and one that my parents certainty did not give to me.

Sometimes I wonder if my brother and sister ever think of me. I wonder what their lives are like? Are they struggling? They probably are because my parents showed them how to struggle and to be content with just getting by on the bare minimum. I wonder if my parents are still struggling although all of their children are now grown. I just wonder. I have never picked up the phone or a newspaper to see how they are doing. It's not that I don't care, but I can't forgive them for bringing children into this world and not being able to provide them with a good life. I just wonder what has become of them, but my curiosity is not strong enough for me to find out.

I'm simply happy with the man that I have now. Terrance is even more to me than the last guy that I was engaged to marry. He would have been perfect too had he not tried to investigate my past. He came really close to discovering my identity, but I put a stop to that. It was the night that I discovered he had newspapers from my hometown. I'm not sure why or how he did his research, but it was too close for comfort. I asked him to meet me on this beautiful mountain called "Top of Green Mountain." He and I used to go there often when we were first dating. The area was secluded, and the view was that of the entire city. He agreed to meet me there because I told him that I had something on my mind that I had wanted to share with him for quite some time. I'm sure he thought I was there to confess my true identity. I just never understood why he never asked me. Once there, I did confess to him my version of the truth. I could have left it there because he believed what I told him. He even said he was more in love with me for being honest. We kissed, but it was something about the kiss that felt different. I didn't trust him. His back was facing the rail. I was so passionate that he didn't notice that I was leading him to the edge. It was too late when he realized it. He opened his eyes to look at me when he realized that I had pushed him over. I leaned over to watch him hit the bottom. I gathered my composure and drove away as if nothing had happened. The next morning his death was ruled a suicide. No one ever thought to look twice at me, and his family accepted that there was something in his life that he was keeping a secret and could no longer handle. They knew he had something on his mind, but little did they know the secret he was keeping was my secret. My true identity.

CHAPTER 21

News

Several people in the office were gathered around the TV in the break room to hear the breaking news that Grant had passed after being in a coma for three weeks. Terrance remained in his office because he was too consumed with his new role. He was working longer hours while Priyanka was taking a lot of time off handling last minute wedding plans.

People in the office were saddened to hear the news that Grant had passed away. They were pulling for him despite their not knowing him personally. He and his family were well liked because of their contributions to the community. Priyanka went along with the emotions of everyone in the room. Silently, she was relieved that Grant had died because her secret also died.

Later that night, Terrance decided to watch the news to see what everyone was talking about in the office. He was not one to watch the news or to read the newspapers if it didn't have anything to do with his clients. He mostly read law publications or business articles.

"Baby, are you watching the news tonight?" asked Priyanka as she entered the bedroom to find Terrance sitting on the edge of the bed watching TV.

"Yes. Have you heard anything about this Grant guy? There was so much talk today in the office that I decided to watch tonight. Have you heard anything about it?"

"A few weeks ago it was all over the news that he had been shot in the chest. Remember, you insisted that I turn from the news because it was too depressing?"

"Oh yes. I do remember, but do they know who shot him?" asked Terrance.

"Baby, I don't know. No one knows. They found him in his condo alone. Are you trying to play detective? Why are you concerned anyway?"

"I'm not concerned, but it is interesting. It has to be someone he knows or trusts enough to let into his place."

"I'm not sure, but his family has enough money to find whoever did this to him. Now, can we please turn to a different channel? As you said, it's depressing, and I can't believe all the media coverage this guy is getting. I'm sure it's because he comes from a wealthy family."

"If I didn't know you better, I would say you have no compassion for this guy or his family."

"Baby, you know I care. I just hate how the media sensationalizes tragedies. They couldn't care less about this man. All they care about are their ratings."

"You're right, but I think it's still a sad situation."

Pointing the remote to the television, Terrance changed the TV to a different channel. Priyanka was relieved because all the conversation about Grant was making her uncomfortable.

JAYLAN

Jaylan entered his bedroom to find his wife working at the computer while the television was on. The local news was on, and Jaylan was not paying any attention to it. He reached for the remote located on the table next to the television to turn the television off, but as he reached for the remote, he saw a big picture of Grant flash across the screen.

"I know that guy!" yelled Grant.

"What guy?" asked Melody as she turned from the computer to see who Jaylan was talking about.

"Oh that's the guy whose been all over the news. He was shot and killed in his apartment. I doubt if you know him."

"No, I know this guy. I just can't remember where I know him from."

"Was he a client?"

"I don't recall, but I've seen him somewhere."

"It has to be work related."

"Could be, but I doubt it. I normally don't forget clients or people that I have worked with."

"Apparently, he is well-liked, so maybe you just read about him and think you saw him somewhere. I read on the internet today that he comes from a well-to-do family and that he's originally from Wisconsin," stated Melody.

"He must have done a lot for him to be all over the news. I feel bad for his family. Do they have any leads?"

"No, I read they found him in his condo with gunshot wounds to the chest. He must have known the person to have let them into his condo. Apparently, he didn't call his wife to let her know he was staying at his condo that night. She was worried and had security check in on him; that's when they found him lying in a pool of blood. There is speculation that he may have been having an affair, but they have found no evidence of an affair."

"Too bad, but whoever did it will get caught. There's no such thing as a perfect crime," replied Jaylan as he aimed and clicked the remote control to turn off the television.

CHAPTER 22

Charlene and Terrance

Charlene called Terrance to tell him that she was going to be in town and would love to meet him for dinner. Charlene had not had a chance to meet with Terrance alone since their chance meeting nearly six months ago. She had been talking with Priyanka nearly every week in regard to the wedding. But now that the wedding was only a couple of weeks away, Charlene wanted to spend some time with Terrance alone. Terrance was happy to hear from Charlene and agreed to meet her for dinner while she was in town.

Terrance didn't tell Priyanka that he was meeting Charlene for dinner. He decided not to say anything because he did not want Priyanka to get the wrong idea about his relationship with Charlene. He knew that Priyanka was consumed with the finishing touches on the wedding and would assume that he was working late at the office.

He agreed to meet Charlene at a restaurant close to his office. He didn't want to travel as far as the hotel where Charlene was staying.

Terrance arrived at the restaurant before Charlene so he waited for her at the bar.

His thoughts were disturbed a few minutes later by a soft spoken but familiar voice.

"Excuse me handsome but is someone sitting here?"

"Hey beautiful. I was saving it for someone special."

They both looked at each other and laughed out loud at their joking with each other.

"How are you? I wanted to spend a little time with my friend before he walks down the aisle."

"I hear you. There's a table over there in the corner. Let's see if we can sit there," replied Terrance

The waitress led them over to the empty table that Terrance had requested. He pulled the seat out for Charlene and ordered a glass of wine for him and Charlene.

"So, tell me Mr. T, how have you been? Are you ready for your big day? I've been talking to Priyanka nearly every week but have not had a chance to have a one-on-one with you."

"It has been crazy with my new role at work and with the wedding. I will say that Priyanka is holding it all together. She's amazing at planning. She keeps me organized."

"Sounds like you are marrying the right woman."

"Yes, I believe so. I really feel that she's the one for me."

Terrance was saying one thing but his body language was saying something different.

"Hmmm, sounds like I detect a little apprehension in your voice. Is there uncertainty going on? Cold feet?"

"No, I would not call it uncertainty. I just want it to be perfect. I just want Priyanka to know how much I love her. I will admit that at times I don't think she knows, and I wonder if I'm doing something wrong."

"Why do you say that?"

"I'll tell you this, but you have to promise not to ever repeat this-- especially in front of Jaylan."

"You can trust me. I won't say anything. I just want you to be happy."

"I am happy, but there was one time that Priyanka did something that really bothered me. She saw me in the break room at work talking to a couple of my female co-workers. Charlene, she was so rude to them that it was embarrassing. I don't think I have ever been as embarrassed. The ladies were nice and quietly left Priyanka and me in the break room."

"What did you say to Priyanka about her behavior?"

"I never got the chance to say anything to her about it because, let's just say, she had other plans when I got home that night. I could see that she was embarrassed about her behavior and she felt bad, so I just let it go. It has stayed in the back of my mind, though"

Charlene sat there and listened as she was recalling how Priyanka was rude to her in the same matter. She wondered if she should mention it to Terrance but then thought it was pointless because she knew Terrance was still going to marry Priyanka.

"Terrance, she was probably feeling a little threatened, which is normal. She has found herself a great man, so she wants to be sure it stays that way. Maybe she saw that they were flirting. Men have a tendency not to notice such behavior."

"Could be, but I don't think so. My co-workers and I were actually talking about my wedding, but if you say so. You and Priyanka are women; you know better than I do."

"Yes, but just be truthful with Priyanka if it happens again. Tell her how you really feel. She will never know if you're not honest with her. If she has jealousy issues, then they will only get worse."

"Sounds like you are speaking from experience."

"No, I'm not at all. I've never been in a jealous relationship, but I do know you should be honest with Priyanka if something bothers you. Otherwise, you'll have to put up with it throughout your marriage."

"I hear you. So, tell me why you aren't married?"

"I'm not sure. I had some pretty good relationships but nothing to take to the next level. To be honest with you, I do know why I'm not married. I've put all my energy into my career, and I think it has a lot to do with the death of my mother. My mother was everything to me. I lived to make her proud. I feel that I have no one who would be as excited to see me walk down an aisle in a beautiful wedding dress as my mother would if she was here. I don't have anyone rushing me to have grandchildren. I have my aunt, but she's not my mother. I'm sure she loves me, but it does not feel like the love I felt with my mother. I could go on and on Terrance, but I think you get the point."

"I hear you Charlene, but I think you are overlooking the fact that once you find the right person, you will know, and that person will fill the void in your life. You are such a cool, caring person that I know that special person would welcome you into their family and provide you with the love you feel you are missing. You'll never feel that mother-to-daughter love you felt with your mother, but you'll find a different kind of love--a special love that will ease the pain of losing your mother. Right now, you feel that you can't give love because you miss your mother so much, but trust me, it will get better."

"You are right. You are giving me something to consider. There is a guy that I'm seeing, but I have not opened up to him as much as he deserves. I had considered bringing him to the wedding. I may just bring him now that you have me thinking differently."

Terrance and Charlene had talked for a couple of hours before either of them realized the time. Terrance made the statement that he better be getting home because he knew that Priyanka would have something for him to do regarding their wedding. Terrance did take to heart the advice he received from Charlene. He had planned on not telling Priyanka that he was with Charlene, but he had a change of heart and decided that his dinner with Charlene was innocent and there was nothing to hide. He was ready to be open with Priyanka regardless of her reaction.

Priyanka was home and had not thought to call Terrance to see if he was in the office. She assumed he was working and had prepared dinner for him.

Priyanka greeted Terrance with a kiss as he entered the house.

"Hey baby, you look tired. I made dinner for you. You've been working so hard lately that I know you have to be tired. What are they going to do without you when we are on our honeymoon?"

"They'll be fine without me because I'm working longer hours to be sure that I don't leave anything hanging, but don't forget, they will call me if necessary. I hate it, but it comes along with the job."

"I know, but hopefully they will be able to manage without you. Go change and I'll put dinner on the table for you."

"Baby, I've already eaten. Charlene was in town and called to see if I could meet her for dinner. I should have called you, but I knew you would be busy with the wedding. I didn't want you to feel like you had to make time to have dinner with us. Have you eaten? I'll sit at the table with you and keep you company."

"Terrance, I haven't eaten. I was waiting on you. I can't believe you didn't call me. Why are you so secretive when it comes to Charlene? It makes me think you have feelings for her or something? Do you Terrance? Do you have something you want to tell me? What is it about this Charlene? I don't see what you see in her. I thought I was over reacting when it came to her, but I really believe that she is trying to come between us. We will be married in two weeks, and she is trying to stop that from happening!"

Priyanka immediately ran to the bedroom after expressing her disappointment with Terrance for having dinner with Charlene.

Terrance ran behind her. He wanted to be sure that he addressed Priyanka's reaction. He wanted her to understand that there was nothing between He and Charlene.

Priyanka had her head buried in the pillow.

"Baby, calm down. There is nothing between Charlene and me. We are just friends. I should have called you to let you know that I was having dinner with her, but to be honest with you I didn't tell you for this very reason. I love you Baby, but you scare me when you show these jealous tendencies. I don't like it Baby. It scares me. I don't want this to be a part of our marriage. Can we talk about your fears? Can you tell me why you feel this way? I've done everything to include you in my life. Charlene is a friend and nothing more. I wouldn't be able to tell you one thing about those women in the break room that you reacted rudely to. I know nothing about them and don't care to know. They were simply carrying on a friendly conversation about our wedding.

Tell me. What is it that makes you act this way?"

Priyanka rose up from the pillow and sat with her legs Indian style as she responded to the questions Terrance had.

"I don't know, Baby. I just don't want to lose you. I'm sorry. I promise it won't happen again, but you have to be honest with me. You can't hide things from me. All you had to do was to tell me that you were having dinner with Charlene. I like Charlene. She's a good girl, but when you do what you did today, you make me think you have romantic feelings for her. I don't have an excuse for the women in the break room. I know women are going to flirt with you. I honestly trust you. I'm sorry baby. Can you forgive me?" Priyanka moved closer to Terrance and placed her head on his shoulder.

Terrance took her into his arms and told her that she had nothing to worry about when it came to other women because no one could take her place.

CHAPTER 23

Priyanka

What am I going to do? Things are getting out of control. I thought everything was under control when I found out that Grant had passed. It was a great day for me. My comfort has now been replaced with the actions of Charlene. She is after my man and has to be stopped. How dare she plan a secret dinner with Terrance? I had just spoken to her two days ago. She never mentioned that she was coming to town. She never told me that she was going to call my man. I can't trust her. I can never trust her around my husband. She's not going away for sure. Terrance adores her, and I'm sure he's in love with her and doesn't know it. It's only a matter of time. I have to find a way to make her disappear. What can I do? At this point, I don't even want her in my wedding. I can't tell Terrance because I would definitely lose him if I show any more signs of jealousy when it concerns Charlene or anyone else for that matter. I have to find a way to make her disappear.

When I got to the office today, I saw that Terrance's assistant was already there. She was on the computer on the Internet. I walked in to say hello and to give her a wedding invitation. I wanted to give it to her personally because I know she's not as happy as she pretends to be about Terrance and me. I asked her what she was reading. She told me that she was reading about Grant. Apparently, about his funeral which was front-page news again. I smiled and told her that I hope she will be able to make it to my wedding.

I walked over to my desk and signed on to my computer. I did something that I have not done in fifteen years. All of this talk about Grant had me thinking about my parents. I thought about searching for them to see what they were doing with themselves. I typed my father's name in the search field three times and back spaced three times to erase his name before I hit the enter key. The fourth time that I typed his name I hit enter instead of back spacing. Several lines appeared but the one that stood out was an obituary. I clicked that line description. As the little hourglass sat in the middle of the computer, my heart raced. I had visions of my father's face the day that he and my mother visited me in the hospital when I brought Justin into the world. I saw the pain he felt when I didn't have much to say to them or when I told them that I named my son after someone in Mark's family. I saw the hurt when I treated him like he was nothing because he didn't have money or the job I thought he should have had. As I waited for the information to appear and the hourglass to disappear I remembered all the times I treated him badly. The information finally appeared. I read that he died on the job due to faulty equipment. As a result, the company settled out of court with his wife, my mother, for an undisclosed amount of money.

I couldn't help the way I felt about my parents then, and I'm not about to start beating myself up over it now just because he's dead. I think I did a good thing by getting out of their lives. I would have only made them more miserable than I had because they never understood why I wanted more out of life. They simply never understood, and I don't feel bad about that. I'm sure my mother is doing well now and that makes me happy. I hate my father had to lose his life, but life goes on. Ironically, his death afforded him an opportunity to finally give my mother the life she deserved. When a man marries a woman, he should be able to give her a good life.

I couldn't do a search for my mother. I've already gone against what I said that I would never do and that is to look back, but all of this Grant stuff aroused my curiosity. I have to get my thoughts back to figuring out what to do about Charlene.

CHAPTER 24

Closer

Jaylan passed a newspaper stand as he walked to his office building from where he parked. On the front page was a picture of Grant. Jaylan stopped and decided to pick up a copy. There was something about Grant's face that was familiar to him, but he still had not figured why he felt he knew Grant. He folded the newspaper and placed it in his briefcase, intending to read it during his lunch hour or take it home to read after work.

Two days later when Jaylan was home cleaning out his briefcase, he saw the newspaper and remembered that he had purchased it to read the story. Melody was sitting on the sofa next to Jaylan as he read the paper.

"Damn! I knew that I knew this guy from somewhere!" He continued to read.

"What are you talking about?"

"Remember the other day when I told you I knew this guy from somewhere?" replied Jaylan pointing to the picture of Grant on the front page.

"Yes, but where do you know him from?"

"This is the guy that I saw pulling on Priyanka's arm."

"Shut up! I do remember, but he was mistaken, right? He didn't really know her."

"According to him and Priyanka he was mistaken. But it was just weird to me. I felt like they knew each other. I felt that something was not right. Priyanka just didn't seem like she was shaken. Think about it. If a man walks up to you to see if you are someone else, he's not going to grab your arm, and if he does you are going to scream out for help, right? Priyanka just walked away and told me to forget about it and not to worry Terrance."

"Yes, that is weird. But still, what does that incident have to with his death?"

"Nothing, I hope, but just knowing more about him may lead me to Priyanka's past. I still believe she is hiding something. Here it says he is from some small town in Wisconsin. I'll start there."

"What do you mean? What are you talking about? Are you going to play detective now, or have you just lost your mind?"

"Yes, I need to know who this woman is, and I need to know as soon as possible. The wedding is only a couple of weeks away. There is something not right with Priyanka, and I'm going to try my best to find out."

"Baby, I think you should leave this alone. Terrance knows what he is doing, and how do you think he will react when he finds out you are investigating Priyanka and you promised him that you wouldn't?"

"What I'm about to do is between you and me. I'll just take two days off from work and go to Wisconsin to check it out. All you have to do is to say that I'm away on business."

"Do what you have to do but promise me you will be careful."

CHAPTER 25

Charlene

Charlene was preparing to leave for work when she received a call from Priyanka asking her if she could join her on an overnight trip to Maine. She went on to explain that she wanted it to be a surprise to Terrance.

"Why Maine?"

"Maine is so beautiful, and they have some of the most beautiful beaches in the world. Terrance loves the beach. Everyone goes to California and Florida. I want to surprise him with something different. We have never been to a beach in Maine, and it's not too far. Because of Terrance's commitments at work, we only have a few days for our honeymoon, so I think this place will be perfect."

"Why do you need me?"

"Charlene, you're one of Terrance's best friends, and I just need a second opinion. Besides, it will give us one last chance to get to know each other."

"What beach is it?"

"I want it to be a surprise to you as well. Just trust me and say you will join me."

"I guess I could get away for a day but not any longer. I've already taken off for the wedding."

"Great! I'll make all the arrangements and call you back with the information. I'm so excited!"

That was easy. Now that she is going to meet me, all I have to do is to make her disappear while in Maine. I don't want to kill her, but what else can I do? I just need to detain her until Terrance and I are married. Maybe I'll just tie her up and keep her there. I can visit her from time to time to keep her alive. But where would I keep her without anyone knowing? I don't know! Why is life so hard? I just want Terrance and me to have a perfect life," thought Priyanka as she thought of what to do with Charlene once in Maine.

CHAPTER 26

Jaylan goes to Wisconsin

J aylan's first stop was the main library in town where his research led him to Grant's family. He found that Grant's family was well-respected and lived in a small town called Ephraim which was located about an hour from the hotel where Jaylan was staying.

Jaylan called Melody to let her know where he was staying. He told her that he had found Grant's parents and was going to see them the following morning to see if they knew Priyanka.

Luckily, Grant's parent's phone number was listed. He called and asked if he could stop by to speak with them the following morning. Grant's father hesitated to give him permission to visit, but when Jaylan told him that he had run into Grant in New York, he agreed to see him. Grant's parents were more than anxious to speak with Jaylan after learning that Jaylan had seen their son in New York. They were hopeful that Jaylan would have information that would lead to finding the person responsible for their son's death. They wanted to know more. They wondered if Grant had a separate life that no one close to him knew about.

Jaylan arrived the following morning as planned. Mrs. Cort, Grant's mother, welcomed him into her home after Jaylan appeared at her doorstep.

"Please come in. My husband is waiting for you in the study."

"Thank you for agreeing to meet with me, and I'm so sorry for your loss."

Mrs. Cort led him to the room where her husband was waiting. Jaylan entered the room to see a man with a striking resemblance to the stranger he once met on the street.

"Hello, Mr. Cort, thank you for taking time to meet with me. I only met your son once, but I will say that the two of you could pass for twins."

Jaylan was uncomfortable and nervous.

"No problem, son, but what can we do for you. My wife and I have been trying to figure out why you would come all this way from New York to talk to us? Why would you want to meet with us when you didn't even know our son?"

"Gosh, where do I start? Two or three months ago, I was uptown in New York where I believe your son's office is located?"

"Yes," replied Mr. Cort

"I sort of met him there. He was having what looked to be a heated conversation with a woman that I know. He was pulling on her arm as she tried pulling away. Without hesitation, I intervened because I felt she was in danger. She told me it was a misunderstanding and that he thought she was someone else. He agreed. To be honest with you, I didn't believe either of them. I felt they knew each other and were having an argument about something. I could be wrong but that's why I'm here."

"That does not sound like Grant, handling someone in that manner, especially a woman," replied Mrs. Cort.

"With all due respect, Mrs. Cort, I didn't know your son, so I can't say. All I know is what I saw. They were having a heated conversation, but both eventually denied knowing each other."

"Who is the woman, and why don't you have these questions for her?" asked Mr. Cort.

"It's awkward to say the least. She's the fiancée of my best friend. They will be married in a couple of weeks. I don't think she is being honest about who she is, so I'm trying to do my own investigation."

"So, are you implying there was something romantically between her and Grant?" asked Mr. Cort.

"No, I'm just simply looking for answers. I just thought I would be able to find some answers here."

"Son, we are not looking to hurt my daughter-in- law. Let's assume he had something going on with this woman. How is that going to help any of us? The media would be all over it. There are already speculations that he was having an affair. We don't need nor; do we want that type of attention. We need to know who is responsible for Grant's death."

"May I ask you a question?" asked Mrs. Cort.

"Of course."

"Do you think this woman may have been the person who shot Grant?"

"Mrs. Cort, I absolutely don't believe so. I can't see her doing something so cold. I'm sorry to have bothered you and your husband. I guess I was looking for answers in the wrong place." Jaylan stood and motioned to leave.

"Wait, do you have a picture of this girl? Grant has never said anything to us about another woman. Maybe she's a co-worker?" asked Mrs. Cort.

"No, she's not a co-worker. I wish I had, but I didn't think to bring a photo."

"Honey, why are you going there? I've already told him that we have no idea what Grant and this woman were discussing. We don't need to see a photo."

"Wait! I do have the wedding invitation in the car. It has a picture of her on it. Jaylan hurried out the door to the car.

He returned with the invitation and placed it on the table where they both could see.

"Hmm, she's a beautiful girl, but I don't think we know her. I thought you were talking about a white woman. I'm sure there was nothing between the two of them. What's her name?" asked Mrs. Cort

"Priyanka Depesh. Priyanka Depesh," answered Jaylan in a defeated tone.

"Can you leave this with us? We'll ask around. Maybe someone from Grant's high school will know her," stated Mrs. Cort.

"Sure. I was hoping to have some information before I returned home."

Mrs. Cort felt bad for Jaylan and wanted to help anyway she could. She told Jaylan she would ask one last person before she sent him away feeling defeated. She could hear defeat in his tone of voice and see defeat in the expression on his face.

"Let me call Meredith. She's a good friend of Grant's. Maybe she will know something."

Mr. Cort watched his wife and wanted to intervene to avoid giving Jaylan false hope, but he was willing to let his wife give it another try before he said anything further.

Jaylan waited patiently as Mrs. Cort called Meredith.

Meredith answered the phone and immediately asked if everything was ok and if they had any updates about what had happened to Grant. Mrs. Cort informed her that Jaylan was at her home and was asking about a girl that Grant may have known. She asked Meredith if she knew whether or not Grant had been friends with an African American woman from high school?

"Grant had many friends in high school that were African American females. What does she look like?"

"Excuse me Ms. Cort but she's not African American. She's actually Indian. She's from India."

"Oh, I apologize. Meredith, did you hear the young man?"

"Yes, the only person I can think of is Natalie Coleman. She is African American, but a lot of people thought she was Indian. She was very beautiful."

"Thank you Meredith. You've been very helpful. I don't think we are talking about the same person."

"Not a problem. Please don't hesitate to let me know if there is something that I can do for you and your family. Losing Grant is such a loss."

"You're sweet. Take care, and I will talk to you soon."

"Oh, Mrs. Cort, I just thought of something. You can look in one of Grant's old year books to see if the girl is Natalie Coleman. Remember, she was the girl that disappeared with her son and was never founded."

"Honey, can you pull out one of Grant's old year books? Meredith just reminded me of something."

Mr. Cort went to the back room and returned with a yearbook from Grant's senior year.

They flipped through the pages and there on the second page of the junior section was Priyanka standing and smiling with a caption reading "most likely to succeed".

Mr. and Ms. Cort could see from the expression on Jaylan's face that Natalie Coleman was the same girl he thought to be someone else.

"Are you ok, son?" asked Mr. Cort.

"Yes sir I am. I just can't figure out why she would lie about who she is and what else is she hiding."

"Wait! Do you think she may have had something to do with the death of my son?" asked Mrs. Cort,

"Mrs. Cort, please give me a few days before you say anything to anyone. I need to figure this out. I don't want to alarm anyone, and I certainly don't want to run her off. To answer your question, after finding this out, I honestly don't know what she is capable of."

"We understand, but do we need to get a private investigator or perhaps get the police involved?" asked Mr. Cort

"That would be great, but I don't want you to get your hopes up. This may have nothing to do with the death of your son."

"That's a chance we are willing to take. Leave us your information, and we will be in touch. All we ask is that you work with the private investigator," stated Mr. Cort.

CHAPTER 27

Terrance Thoughts

"Things are moving fast. I know that Priyanka is the right girl for me, but she has been so distant lately. I wonder if she is having second thoughts. My mother told me that most females second guess their decision when they are about to get married. I want Priyanka to know that there is nothing in this world that I would not do for her. She is my life, and I thank God every day for blessing me with her. Here I am, a boy from Alabama moved to New York, lands the perfect job and now a perfect wife. I don't think any man could ask for more. I have to do something special for her when she returns from her secret trip. She says she is planning something special for the two of us. I wish I had more time for our honeymoon, but I'm sure she has located the perfect place for us and is making sure everything is perfect. I can feel that life is going to be an adventure with her, and there will never be a dull moment. She is truly a wonderful woman."

CHAPTER 28

Jaylan's Thoughts

"What do I do with this information? I can't tell Terrance. I don't want to burden my wife with this information? Who can I tell? What should I do?"

Jaylan walked back to his car with his head hanging down. He was disturbed by what he had found out about Priyanka. He was saddened by the truth that his friend was in love with a woman who did not exist. He wanted to know more. He wanted to know if there was a reason why Priyanka changed her identity. He thought maybe it had something to do with her family and that she was hiding from them. He decided to go back to the library to see if he could find anything on Priyanka by using her true name of Natalie Coleman.

Jaylan sat at a computer in the corner of the library. He hesitated typing in the name of Natalie Coleman. His mind kept wondering back to Terrance. He didn't know how he was going to tell Terrance about Priyanka. Mostly, he feared that Terrance would not want to hear what he had to say.

Placing his head on the desk momentarily, Jaylan thought that maybe Priyanka had a good reason for changing her identity.

Placing his fingers back on the keyboard, Jaylan typed in the name Natalie Coleman. There appeared before his eyes multiple articles on a missing girl by the name of Natalie Coleman. Jaylan spent nearly three hours in the library reading all of the articles. Through the articles, he learned that Natalie had a baby boy, and they both went missing. The article listed all the information on how to reach her parents. The picture was becoming clearer to Jaylan, but he felt he had to speak with her parents.

Jaylan arrived at the address listed in the article. It was a ranch home. The yard was so well landscaped that it looked like a historical site for touring. Jaylan walked up four steps leading to the front door of the home. The front door was open, so he could see through the glass screened door. He rang the doorbell, but no one answered. He put his face closer to the door to see if he could see someone inside. He decided to walk around to the back of the house after waiting for approximately three minutes. He stepped on the concrete path leading to the back of the house. Once he reached the back of the house, he saw an older woman kneeling planting flowers and a few feet away, there was an older man sitting in a wheel chair staring straight with little control of his arms.

"Excuse me, are you Mrs. Coleman?" Jaylan walked closer to the woman, surprised to see the resemblance to Priyanka when she turned to face him that he was almost speechless.

"Yes, I am. How may I help you?" Mrs. Coleman asked in a curious tone.

"Do you have a few minutes to talk to me?"

"Sir, I don't mean to be rude, but what is it that you need to talk to me about? I don't believe I know you?"

"No, you don't know me, and I apologize for coming to you in this manner. I don't want to alarm you, but I do want to ask you about your daughter, Natalie."

Mrs. Coleman dropped the planting instrument she was holding in her hand. She stood up and walked over to the guy in the wheel chair. She stood behind the wheel chair and started to push it towards the home when she asked Jaylan to follow her.

Once in the house she took the man in the wheel chair to another room and closed the door. She walked back out to the room where she had left Jaylan. Jaylan was looking at the pictures around the room when she returned.

"Did you say you have information on my daughter, Natalie?"

"Maybe, I'm not sure. I know a girl who claims she is someone else, but I have reason to believe she is Natalie."

"Please tell me what you know. My daughter and my grandson have been missing for fifteen years. My husband passed away a couple of years ago. Each year before his accident, he would travel to a different state searching for Natalie. He never gave up."

"If the person I believe to be your daughter is your daughter then she lives in New York and goes by the name of Priyanka Depesh. She tells everyone that she is from Mumbai India. I don't mean to be disrespectful, Mrs. Coleman but why would she do something like that? Was she abused?"

"No, no abuse whatsoever. We have two other children who can attest to that. My husband and I always provided the best we could for our children who are all grown now. Natalie is the oldest, and she was never satisfied with what we had. She wanted more. She wanted a big beautiful home like some of the people she went to high school with. She wanted us to have more, but we did the best we could. It was just never enough for Natalie."

"When did she leave?"

"She left us while she was a senior in high school. She became extremely disrespectful towards my husband and me."

"Did you and your husband put her out of your home?"

"We absolutely did not and would never have done such a thing even when she spoke to us like we were nothing. She got pregnant and decided she wanted to live with the father of her baby and his family. Mark, the father of her child is a nice person and was funding those trips that my husband took to look for Natalie. He went with my husband as often as he could, but by his being a professional football player, his time was limited. Even with all the money he has, he has never been able to locate Natalie and Justin. I don't know how many trips he has taken since my husband passed away. I don't hear from him much now. My husband was the driving force to continue to look for her. I guess you can say we all gave up when he passed away. I don't know what to feel knowing that she's alive and never bothered to contact us. There was a time when I felt really guilty about not being there emotionally for my other children because I was so heartbroken over Natalie. But they all tell me to this day not to feel guilty because they understood. They turned out to be wonderful people. I don't mean to go on and on and take up your time, but I've always known that Natalie was living somewhere and didn't want to be found. She left Mark and his family the same way she left our family. I'm really not surprised to hear the things you are telling me.

"I'm sorry to hear that, Mrs. Coleman; it seems like you and your family have been through a lot. I didn't mean to bring back bad emotions. Priyanka is fine, but there is no child. She has never indicated anything about a child, and I'm sure of that. She's about to be married to my friend in a couple of weeks which is why I'm here. I've never trusted her, but not in a million years would I have suspected all of this. I don't know how I'm going to break this news to my friend, but I have to. I'm still having a hard time understanding why she would do what she has? She has to be hiding something more severe, something that you may not be aware of. The son should be fifteen now, right?"

"Yes," replied Mrs. Coleman

"Thank you so much for talking to me. I'm trying to pull all the pieces together. I will be in touch when I have more information. Please do not try to contact her. You'll only make her run away again. I promise that I will be back in touch with you. I'll leave my number in case you need to speak with me."

"Wait, do you think she may have killed her son?"

"I don't know, but I'm positive that Natalie and Priyanka are the same person. It's a long story about how I know, but a private investigator is working on the details. I have to get back to New York, but I will definitely be in touch with you."

"Thank you for stopping by. I hope to see my daughter soon. No matter what she has done or how badly she has treated us, there is still a part of me that wants to see and hug her as if she was the little girl who walked away from us." Mrs. Coleman led Jaylan to the door and watched him get into his vehicle.

CHAPTER 29

Priyanka's Thoughts

"Now that my wedding date is two weeks away, and I have my plan in motion to remove Charlene from the picture, I'm starting to get really excited again about marrying Terrance. Terrance's family will be here next week. Here I am in Maine waiting on Charlene to show up and thinking about the son I left here fifteen years ago. I wouldn't know where to begin to look for him, even if I wanted to. He should be happy considering I left him with a family that had the means that all parents should have. No one should bring a child into the world unless they are able to give them a good life. My parents were wrong to bring not one, but three children into this world knowing they both had blue collar jobs and could barely afford the mortgage. Thinking back, I don't feel bad that I left them and have never looked back. I do hope that my siblings were able to figure out how to make good lives for themselves, as I have. I'm sure in their eyes I'm a monster because of what I put my parents through. I just never felt the need to know what's going on in their lives. Charlene will be here soon. My plan is to lead her to the top of the lighthouse and push her over. The attendant told me that tonight will be a slow night with very few tourists which will be my opportunity to push her over. I have no other alternative but to make her go away. I only told her I was considering a beach just to get her to agree to come here. What else can I do? I can't lock her in a room and expect her to stay there. I have to make it so it won't interfere with our wedding which is why I must do it today. Terrance will have two weeks to grieve. He wouldn't dare put our wedding on hold just because she's gone."

CHAPTER 30

Charlene Arrives

Charlene didn't bother to tell anyone where she was going because she had planned on returning the very next morning. Priyanka had arranged for a car to pick her up from the airport and to drop her off at the hotel where the room was registered under Priyanka's name.

Charlene entered the hotel room to find Priyanka sitting on the bed all dressed waiting to leave.

"Hey girl, you seem ready to go."

"I am. We have very little time."

"Do we at least have time for dinner? I'm starved. I went straight to the airport from work and didn't get a chance to have lunch."

"Charlene, the tour is about 15 minutes long. We can eat afterwards. I want to be sure we make it on time, so you can see it all. I really need your help in deciding. The site is beautiful from the lighthouse. I know you're going to love it."

"Lighthouse? I didn't know we were going to a lighthouse? What happened to the beach? What's romantic about a lighthouse? I agree this is a beautiful city, but I think we can find something more romantic."

"You'll have to see it. You could be right which is why I brought you here for your opinion, but I do want you to see it first. If you don't like it, we can have dinner and look at a couple of other places."

"Sounds like a plan to me. I'm not too sure about a lighthouse and besides, I don't like heights, but if it's what you want I can handle it."

"Don't worry, girl; you'll be fine. I won't let you fall."

There were five people on the tour including Priyanka, and Charlene. The tour started with instructions from the tour guide leading the tour. He joked about the rope surrounding the edge of the railing. "The rope serves as a warning the same as it would in the middle of the ocean except there are no sharks here." No one got the joke. "In other words, don't lean on it." The coastline was rocky, and the lighthouse stood 100 feet above the waters. The winds were high, and the temperature was roughly seventy degrees. It was a tour for adults only. Priyanka wasn't sure how she was going to get Charlene to lean on the rope, but she was sure she had to make it happen.

Charlene looked over at Priyanka as the tour begun. "God, I hate heights. I don't know how I let you talk me into this."

"Girl, relax. You'll be fine. You can hold my hand when the elevator opens if that will make you feel better."

Reaching out for Charlene's hand, Priyanka smiled. Charlene held on to Priyanka's hand tightly as the glass elevator traveled to the top.

Once at the top, the elevator door opened. The winds were strong. The tour guide explained the history of the tower and led the small group of people around to the other side. He reminded the group that they could hold on to the rope if they wanted to but not to lean on it. He was used to people using the rope as comfort and support if they were afraid of heights.

"Look at this beautiful site. How can something so beautiful frighten you?"

Charlene let go of Priyanka's hand and immediately grabbed onto the rope for support. The group had formed a single line as they approached the curve of the tower leading to the other side. Charlene was directly in front of Priyanka. The tour guide and another woman were behind Priyanka. Their view was obstructed so they could not see too far ahead. Priyanka eased closer to Charlene. Moments later she kicked Charlene under her shoe as Charlene moved forward. No one noticed. Charlene was so terrified that she stumbled against the woman in front of her. The woman panicked and grabbed Charlene's arm causing both to lean on the rope. The rope was not strong enough to hold the two women. They both flipped over the rope into the water below.

Priyanka and the woman behind her screamed as they watched Charlene and the other woman fall to the bottom. Rapidly, the tour guide led Priyanka and the rest of the people to the elevator as he called for help from his radio. The rescue squad rushed to the scene to search for Charlene and the other woman. Priyanka and one other woman sat on the back seat of the emergency vehicle wrapped in a blanket shivering from the cold winds. The other woman was the sister of the woman who had fallen with Charlene. Priyanka called Terrance to let him know what was going on.

"Terrance! You have to get here. Something horrible has happened! Please hurry!"

"Priyanka, what are you talking about? Please slow down and talk to me. I don't understand what you are saying!"

"Terrance, there has been an accident. Something terrible has happened to Charlene. I need you to get here as soon as possible. Please come. I need you here!"

Priyanka told Terrance where she was staying and the location of the lighthouse.

CHAPTER 31

Jaylan

Jaylan arrived back in New York the next morning after speaking with Natalie's mother. He was relieved that his wife, Melody, had already left for work when he arrived home. He needed time to think of how he was going to handle telling Terrance what he had found out about Priyanka. He made the decision to tell Terrance what he had found out but worried about the effect it would have on their friendship. He knew his friend's heart would be crushed.

Before Jaylan could reach Terrance, he received a call from the private investigator as promised by Grant's family. The investigator had many questions about Priyanka that Jaylan could not answer. He told the private investigator all that he knew about Priyanka.

He told the private investigator that he was going to tell Terrance what he had found out about Priyanka. The private investigator asked that he hold off telling anyone prior to hearing back from him.

"He is about to be married in a couple of weeks. I can only hold off for one week."

The private investigator assured Jaylan that he would be back in touch with him in a few days.

CHAPTER 32

Maine

Terrance arrived in Maine approximately four hours after speaking with Priyanka. He was not able to get from Priyanka what the problem was over the phone, but on his way to the hotel the taxi driver talked to him about an accident that had occurred at the lighthouse. He explained to Terrance that there were still rescue teams looking for the second woman who had fallen from the top of the lighthouse while on tour. "They found one of the women and rushed her to the hospital. They are still looking for the other one."

Terrance listened to the taxi driver go on and on about the accident, but it never occurred to him that the situation had anything to do with Priyanka and Charlene. He tried reaching Priyanka but was unsuccessful.

Once in the hotel, he asked the desk clerk to call Priyanka's room because he was not able to reach her. The clerk knew what was going on and had been told what to do when Terrance arrived. "Sir, I'm not sure if you have heard but there has been an accident at the lighthouse. Don't worry Ms. Depesh is fine. Security is going to take you to the hospital. Don't worry; she and the other lady were taken to the hospital just for observation."

"Can you tell me more? This is really crazy."

"I'm sorry sir, but this is all the information that I have. You will find out more when you reach the hospital."

When pulling into the hospital's parking lot, Terrance could see there were local and national news reporters waiting to speak to someone to find out more information. Still, Terrance was not able to obtain any information from the security guard who had driven him to the hospital. He led Terrance to a waiting room where other family members of those affected were waiting.

"Can someone please tell me what is going on?" asked Terrance as he entered the waiting room where six other people were waiting.

"You don't know?" asked a woman while wiping tears from her eyes.

"No. My fiancé called me in New York saying that I needed to be here because something terrible had happened."

"If she called you then she must be ok."

"What happened?" asked Terrance.

"There was an accident at the Lighthouse. A couple of people fell from the top during a tour."

"I got that much on my way here."

"Well, they were able to find my cousin. They have not found the other women yet. I suspect your fiancé must be in the other room with the people being questioned by the police."

"Police? I thought it was an accident?" asked Terrance.

"I guess it's just formality. The good news is that your finance is ok. I feel bad for the other woman. They have not been able to find her, and no one has shown up here for her. She has to be dead at this point," stated the woman.

"Oh my God! The other woman has to be Charlene. I remember my fiancé saying she was with Charlene. Oh, my God! Please say it isn't so."

Just as Terrance finished his statement, Priyanka and two other people walked into the waiting room where Terrance and others were waiting. Priyanka ran to Terrance crying. Terrance held her in his arms and tried to calm her so that he could find out what happened.

"Baby, calm down. What happened? Where is Charlene? Was she with you?"

"Terrance, that's what I tried to tell you over the phone. Charlene fell from the top. I tried to tell you. They can't find her. They can't find her, and it's entirely my fault!"

"What! Baby, why was she here? Why are you here? How did she fall?"

"She was here for me. She came here to help me find the perfect place for our honeymoon. It's my fault Terrance! I should have never asked her to come here. I didn't know she had a fear of heights. How can I ever forgive myself? How can you ever forgive me?"

"Priyanka, listen to me. It's not your fault. No one will blame you. We have to do what's best for Charlene. She may be ok. Let's not assume the worst. Let's go down to the lighthouse to see if they have any more information. Don't give up. Charlene is going to be ok."

They were greeted by several reporters as they exited the hospital. Terrance and Priyanka rushed to get into the car to avoid talking to reporters. Terrance asked the driver to take him and Priyanka down to the lighthouse.

The lighthouse was taped off with yellow tape and no one other than rescue personnel could enter. Terrance tried to explain to the guard that he was a relative of the missing person, but that didn't make any difference. He was told to leave his number and that someone would contact him once they had more information.

They went back to the hotel and planned to stay until they received updates regarding Charlene.

"Relax Baby, Charlene will be ok. We can't assume the worst."

"How can you stay so calm? It's entirely my fault."

"Baby, Baby, please stay calm. Relax. It's not your fault and Charlene is ok. Just stay positive."

Terrance watched the news most of the night hoping for updates while Priyanka slept. He wanted to contact Charlene's aunt but didn't know how to reach her.

He slept on and off in the chair while continuing to watch TV throughout the night. The following morning, He called the number he was given by the attendant at the lighthouse. He was not given any information but was asked to come to the Lighthouse immediately.

"Baby, Baby, get up and get dressed. We have to go to the lighthouse."

"Why? Have they found Charlene?"

"Priyanka, come on now. I don't have any answers. Please let's just get ready."

"Why are you mad at me? I know it's my fault, but I didn't push her over."

Pausing for a moment, Terrance hesitated to comment.

"Baby, right now, it's not about you. It's about Charlene. Now, can we please leave?"

Priyanka had never seen Terrance so direct with her. She didn't say another word because she could see that Terrance was worried about Charlene.

Terrance and Priyanka arrived at the lighthouse and were greeted by several officials. They met in a small room where several police officers and other officials were sitting around a table. They were under the impression that Terrance was a relative. He informed them that he was a close friend and that he did not know how to reach her aunt, but he knew where she worked. The officials explained to Terrance that they were not able to find Charlene and had concluded that she was dead.

"What do you mean you've concluded that she is dead? How can that be when you don't even have a body? She could be anywhere."

"Sir, I'm sorry for your loss. We gave it our all. It's likely that her body will appear in a few days."

Terrance turned to Priyanka and placed his head on her shoulder and cried. Priyanka rubbed his head.

"It's going to be ok, Baby. I promise you it's going to be ok."

The official looked at Priyanka as if they could see that she was not as concerned as she pretended to be.

"Excuse me but you were there, right?" one of the officers asked her.

"Yes. I was there. Why do you ask? I've already spoken to an officer for hours."

"I know. I was asking out of curiosity. How exactly did the two women fall over? This has never happened in the twenty years that I've been on the force. There are numerous tours each year with a lot more people which seems strange that such an accident can happen with so few people."

"Sir, I don't mean to be rude, but are you implying something?" asked Terrance.

"No sir, I'm not. I just find it strange. At any rate, it would be much appreciated if you could pass along these papers to the family. The family may reach us at one of the numbers on the form."

"Thank you, sir, for all that you and your staff have done to find our friend. I will definitely give these papers to the family."

Terrance shook a few hands on his way out. Priyanka, in tears, looked over at the officer questioning her and walked out behind Terrance without saying a word.

"Terrance, how can I ever forgive myself?"

"Baby, let's just stay focused. It was not your fault. It was not anyone's fault. Right now, my mind is with Charlene's aunt. I have to get to her before she hears it from someone else. Once we are back at the hotel, please make arrangements for us to leave today as early as possible, and I'll contact someone on her job. I'm sure they will have her aunt's number. My only comfort in this tragedy is that she is now with her mother," stated Terrance.

After reaching someone on Charlene's job for her aunt's number, Terrance contacted Charlene's aunt. He told her what happened and offered to fly her out to Maine. She told him that she did not see a need to go out to Maine but to send her the papers he received from the officer and she would handle everything else. Terrance was taken by her lack of emotion. It was now clear to him why Charlene never spoke of her aunt. He later called her job back to speak with her boss. He told her boss that he was going to have a memorial for her and would let him know when he had all the information.

"Thank you, Mr. Johnson. I'll pass along the information to everyone here. We all are devastated to say the least. Charlene was really loved around here and will be missed."

Priyanka had arranged for a car to pick them up from the airport. Once they were home, Priyanka didn't know what to say. She kept asking Terrance if he was ok. Terrance kept answering, "yes," but it was not until she looked into his eyes that she could see how sad he was.

"Goodness, I almost forgot. I have to call Jaylan. How could I have forgotten about him? What was I thinking?"

He picked up the phone next to his bed and called Jaylan and asked if he and Melody could come over to their home immediately. Jaylan asked if everyone was ok. Terrance told him yes, but he needed him to come over right away.

Jaylan didn't know what to think, but he and his wife got into the car and hurried over to see what was going on with Terrance.

Priyanka answered the door. Both Jaylan and his wife could see that something was wrong. They could see that Priyanka had been crying. Jaylan wondered if Terrance had found out about Priyanka's true identity.

"Are you ok, Priyanka?" asked Melody.

"No, everything is wrong. Please come on in. Terrance is in the bedroom."

"What's going on Terrance?" asked Jaylan.

"Man, it's bad. It's really bad."

"What's bad? You're not making any sense."

"It's Charlene. She's dead. Man, she's dead."

"Dead, what do you mean? I just spoke to her the other day," replied Melody.

"She and Priyanka were in Maine, and that's where it happened."

"Maine? Why were you and Charlene in Maine?" asked Melody.

"We were there picking out the perfect place for Terrance and my honeymoon."

"Honeymoon in Maine? What could have possibly happened? Will someone please explain? The two of you aren't making any sense," stated Jaylan.

"We were there looking at a place for my honeymoon. Our first stop was the lighthouse. I thought it was a beautiful place, so I asked Charlene to go with me to see what she thought. While we were on tour somehow Charlene tripped and fell into the woman in front of her. Before any of us could do anything, they both fell over the rope."

"Where were you Priyanka? Were you close enough to see what caused her to trip?" asked Melody.

"I was close to her, but I didn't see what caused her to trip. I will say that she was terribly afraid. I was not aware that she was afraid of heights. I was right behind her and there were two people behind me. We can't figure out how it happened. It was just a freak accident. They kept us in a room for several hours trying to figure out what happened."

"Why would Charlene agree to go there knowing she was afraid of heights, and have they said outright that Charlene and the other person are dead?" asked Jaylan.

"Well, they were able to locate the other woman. She's in the hospital in critical condition, but they expect her to live. They could not find

Charlene and have all but said that she is dead and that her body will likely surface in a few days," replied Terrance.

"Oh my God! Has anyone contacted her family? This is just awful. Charlene was such a kind person and a wonderful friend to you Terrance." Melody walked over to comfort Terrance by taking him into her arms.

"To answer your question, Jaylan, I didn't tell Charlene that we were going to the lighthouse until she was in Maine. She agreed once she got there. I thought she was ok, but apparently I was wrong. She must have been scared and hiding it from me."

Jaylan stood taking it all in. He couldn't believe everything he was dealing with. He didn't trust that Priyanka had the facts straight.

"Is it ok if we stay over tonight? I don't want to leave you guys alone tonight," reasoned Jaylan.

"Yes, man, that would be cool. Actually, that would be great," replied Terrance.

The four of them had dinner and listened to Terrance talk about some of his childhood memories of Charlene and her mother. As he talked, Jaylan remembered the box that Priyanka had placed in the back of the closet. He quietly slipped away while the other three talked. He managed to slip the box out of the closet and into the bathroom where he could freely look through the box. He knew he could not explain being in their closet should Terrance or Priyanka catch him. He also knew Priyanka would miss the box if she went into the closet, so he had to hurry to view the contents of the box.

He looked through the box but all that were there were college documents for Priyanka. She had somehow managed to get a college degree in her fake name. He continued to look through the box but was not able to find anything but a number written on a piece of paper. It was a number from Wisconsin. Jaylan slipped the box back into the closet. He stored the number in his phone and went back to join everyone else.

"I can't believe how close we are to the wedding," stated Priyanka.

"Baby, let's not talk about the wedding tonight."

"Why can't we talk about the wedding? I don't think Charlene would want us to stop living. I only knew her for a short time, but I feel she would want us to continue living. Terrance, are you saying you want to put our wedding on hold?"

"I think that would be a great idea," suggested Jaylan.

"No, baby. I'm not saying that. I agree with you. Charlene would not want that. She would want us to continue to live, but I do want to give the night to her. I want us to keep all the focus on her tonight."

"I agree. It should be all about her tonight," replied Melody.

"Jaylan, why would you say we should hold off on the wedding?" asked Priyanka.

"I just thought it would be best considering everything that has happened, but I see where that would present a problem so scratch that thought."

"It's getting late. Let's all just get some rest and regroup tomorrow," replied Terrance

Terrance and Priyanka went to their room, and Jaylan and Melody went to the guest room where they normally slept whenever they stayed over.

The next day they all sat at the kitchen table discussing what to do for the Charlene's memorial. They agreed that the service should be held at the church she attended with her aunt. Once the plans were finalized, Terrance contacted Charlene's boss so that he could pass along the information to her co-workers. Melody contacted Charlene's aunt to give her information about the memorial service. Her aunt reluctantly agreed to attend.

The memorial service was held a week later as planned. Terrance, Jaylan, Priyanka and Melody all drove up together. There were a small group of people from her office who attended along with her boss. Her aunt and some of her cousins also attended. Terrance was the speaker. He spoke of how kind a person Charlene was, and he threw in a few memories of their childhood that made the audience laugh. He ended by saying that he would miss his friend, but he found comfort in know that she was flying as an angel with her mother.

CHAPTER 33

Priyanka

The next day Priyanka told Terrance that she was going to stay home from work because she needed to catch up on some wedding details, and she just needed time alone at home to think. Terrance understood and felt bad that Priyanka felt some responsibility for what happened to Charlene.

As soon as Terrance left for work, Priyanka slipped on a pair of comfortable pants and tank top to lounge around the house. She then went to the entertainment room, a room where Terrance spent a lot of time listening to his music. She sat on the floor next to a stand that was holding several CD's. She pulled out a few to see what Terrance had and what she may be in the mood to listen to. She never understood why Terrance was so into his music. He would buy CD's of an artist that she had never heard of. His favorite was R&B music. Priyanka didn't like listening to it because she feared it would take her mind to a place where she did not want to visit. This particular day, she felt that she was in the mood to listen and hoped that it would help her feel better about what she had done to Charlene. She kept seeing images of Charlene over and over again falling from the lighthouse. It had a different effect on her than when she pushed her first fiancee over the cliff of a mountain or when she shot Grant.

She pulled out the CD of a female artist who she didn't know. She felt it was safe and would not take her to a place where she didn't want to go. She didn't like music that her parents listened to because she didn't want to be reminded of Wisconsin.

She put the CD in and sat on the floor in Indian style with a bottle of red wine. The first song was entitled "Didn't we almost have it all." The sound was soft, but the words were powerful. She knew of Whitney but had never bothered to listen to any of Whitney Houston's music back when it first came out. She picked up the case to read more of the titles, but none were interesting enough for her to switch songs. It was as if the song opened her heart, something that she had never experienced. She pressed re-play and turned the volume up louder. The words really got her to thinking. She saw images of herself as a little girl in the yard with her parents planting flowers. She was smiling and running about the yard. She suddenly remembered that there was a time when she was happy with her parents. She remembered feeling safe, something that she had not felt since those days. She had never been intimate with thoughts of her parents. As the song played, each word touched her heart. She saw images of her mother with tears flowing down her face and her father with a frown of disappointment. It was the day they came to visit her in the hospital when she gave birth to her son. Her thoughts then went to how she treated them and how she rudely dismissed them from her life.

"My parents really did love me and would have given me the world, and all I could do was to criticize them for what they did not have. They did the best they could and now that I think of it, they did well considering the background of their parents. I never thought of that."

Priyanka kept hitting replay as the song played near the end. She enjoyed where the song was taking her. At one point, she stood up and looked into the mirror that was positioned on the wall directly over the stereo system.

"Where is my son? What must he think of me! Mark must hate me! Here he is a professional athlete and has to live with my decision to give our son away. It must haunt him each day knowing that he has the wealth to care for his son but has no idea whether or not his son is alive. And Justin, he has no idea who we are or that we exist. I wonder if they ever told him. Stop! I need to stop! I can't worry about these things. I did what I had to do. My parents, my son, my siblings and Mark were all better off without me in their lives!" Still staring in the mirror, Priyanka continued to talk. "I did them all a favor. I had no other choice but to push my ex-fiancé off that mountain and I had no choice in the matter with Grant. The two of them were out to destroy my life, a life that I've worked hard to obtain. I couldn't just let them destroy it. Terrance is a good man, and I can't lose him. I had a gut feeling that Charlene was up to something. There was something about me that she did not trust, and I knew it no matter how she tried to pretend that she liked me. Am I wrong for feeling the same way about her? I didn't trust her. I didn't like the way she and Terrance looked at each other. It was as if the two of them were in love and didn't know it. I had no choice but to do what I did at the lighthouse. Terrance is already doing better. Pretty soon, Terrance and I will be married, and Charlene will be a distant memory."

Priyanka had re-played the song a dozen times. She reached to hit replay again but noticed Terrance standing at the doorway watching. She immediately stopped the music, stood up and ran to Terrance arms.

"What's wrong baby? Why is the music so loud? Why are you crying?"

"Terrance, I was just thinking about how lucky I am to have found such a wonderful man. You are everything to me. I don't remember life before you. I can't live without you. Please tell me that we will start a family together and grow old together."

"Priyanka, you know that I love you and would never leave you. Where is, this coming from?"

"No place, I just feel blessed and would hate to lose you. Terrance, I never told you this, but I love your family too. I know I have been wrong in the past with judging them but Baby, after meeting your family, I can't help but to love them."

"Priyanka, they love you too. Speaking of which, have you made their hotel reservations for next week?"

"No, I've been so scattered brain that I simply forgot. Let me go do it now. Is anyone staying here with us?"

"No, some were but because of Charlene, plans have changed. You may want to call my mother first to ask her how many rooms they will need for the family."

"Sure. Are you getting excited yet?"

"Of course, I'm excited. I've been excited since the day that I met you. I can't wait to begin life with the woman of my dreams. Baby you are everything and more than I had ever thought I would have in a wife. I hope you know that."

Priyanka kissed him softly on the lips and turned to leave the room to call his mother.

CHAPTER 34

Rehearsal Dinner

J aylan had avoided direct contact with Terrance as much as he possibly
could. He didn't want Terrance to sense that something was on his
mind, and he didn't want to be dishonest if Terrance were to ask him if
something was wrong. Jaylan had patiently waited to hear from the private
investigator. He wanted to know if the private investigator was able to find
out more about Priyanka.

While having dinner with his wife, he received a phone call on his
cell phone. He excused himself from the table and took the call to another
room. He was not ready to share the information with his wife either.

"What was that all about?" asked Melody when Jaylan returned to
the table.

"It was nothing. I just got some disturbing news regarding one of my
cases."

"Jaylan, sounds to me like you are not being honest. What's really
going on? I can feel that you are hiding something from me. You have been
acting strange since you came from Wisconsin. What's going on? What are
you not sharing? You do know you can tell me anything, right?"

"Melody, I'm going to tell you something, but you have to promise not
to have a reaction. You have to promise to keep this to yourself."

"You can trust me baby, but you're scaring me right now. What is it?"

Jaylan's hands went numb. He shook them to get the blood back to
circulating.

"God, where do I start? Terrance has himself in a mess and doesn't even know it. Priyanka is not who she says she is."

"What?" interrupted Melody.

"Let me finish, Baby. I'm going to tell you everything, but please listen without reacting."

"Ok. I'm sorry Baby. I know this has to be hard for you."

"Yes, it is to say the least. Priyanka is actually a girl named Natalie and before you say anything she's not Indian at all. She's just as black as you and I. Priyanka is someone she made up. And get this, she had a baby boy shortly after high school or while she was in high school. So much has happened that I don't recall when she had the baby. She left her family and went to stay with the father of the baby and his family. They must have done something to upset her because she took the baby and disappeared. No one has seen either of them since. The son should be about fifteen now. And get this Baby, the father of her son is Mark Preston."

"Mark Preston? Why does that name sound familiar to me?"

"Baby come on, you know Mark Preston, the professional football player?"

"Oh, yeah right. Damn! She is something else. Did you find out all of this while you were in Wisconsin?"

"Yes, I met her mother, and she pretty much told me everything that I needed to know about Priyanka. Well, I should say Natalie."

"Wow, this is deep."

"Yes, it is. Everyone in her home town thought she and her son were dead at this point. It's been fifteen years, and no one has heard from her."

"Then we should think about it from a different perspective. Why did she leave? Was she being abused or something? I don't get it. People just don't disappear without reason."

"That's just it, Baby. I didn't meet the father of her son, and I didn't meet his family. Her mother did say that the family was nice to Priyanka and treated her well. Apparently, her father was in a bad accident at work and died. His wife received a large settlement. Priyanka probably doesn't even know her father has passed. Her mother still wants to reunite with her. She told me that Priyanka hated her and her husband because they didn't have the financial means to give her the life she wanted."

"This is so sad to hear, but I can see that in Priyanka. And I believe she knows about her father. She wants it all. I can't imagine ever treating my parents like that. I'm sure they did the best they could."

"That's not the worst of the story. The private investigator told me that Priyanka did know Grant."

"Wait! When did you meet with a private investigator?"

"It's a long story, but Grant's parents hired a private investigator to try to find out what happened to their son. They were ultimately the reason I found out Priyanka's true name."

"Grant? Oh, you mean the guy that she claimed she didn't know."

"Yes, remember, he's the very reason I decided to go to Wisconsin. I knew she knew him."

"I'm just trying to digest all of this. This is crazy, sounds like a movie."

"Apparently, Grant had contacted Mark the day that he ran into Priyanka. He wanted to find out from Mark if he had ever found Natalie and his son."

"How do you know that if Grant is dead?"

"The investigator has been tracing his steps before he was shot which led him to Mark's number. He contacted Mark. Mark told the investigator he was surprised to hear from Grant after so many years and even more surprised that Grant was able to get to him. He told the investigator that he told Grant that he had been looking for Natalie and his son up until Natalie's father died. It was then that he accepted that Natalie and his son were probably not alive. Grant then told him not to give up because he had reasons to believe that he knew where Natalie was but wanted to wait until he had concrete information before he said more. The investigator said that Mark didn't give too much thought to it. He thought that Grant was like all the rest of the fans, and when he did not hear back from Grant he put the whole thing out of his head. He had not heard that Grant had been killed."

"Baby, are you saying that you think she killed Grant? And where is the son? Has anyone asked that question?"

"I don't know. The investigator asked me to sit tight because the police and FBI are now involved. Baby, it's getting crazier by the day. I feel an obligation to my friend to tell him what's going on. He is getting married next Saturday. I can't continue to hold these lies from him. I just can't."

"Baby, you can't say anything. You will blow the investigation. Terrance will understand when Priyanka has been exposed. This is really bad."

"I just had another crazy thought."

"What's that?" asked Melody.

"What if she's the cause that Charlene fell from that lighthouse?"

"I think the people up there would have seen it if she had. Charlene's falling was just a freak accident."

"I'm not sure about that. It's just too coincidental. She was threatened by Charlene. I could see that whenever we were in the company of the three of them. And remember Charlene told us how Priyanka went off on her in the bathroom. I don't put anything past her. Where is her poor son? Imagine that father having to live not knowing?"

"That's a good question. All we can do at this point is to wait and be there for Terrance when all the chips fall," replied Melody.

CHAPTER 35

Week of the Wedding

I t was the week of the wedding. Priyanka had arranged for Terrance's family to be picked up from the airport and dropped off at the hotel. Terrance paid for everyone's hotel stay but made it clear to them all that they were responsible for their own meals and extra activities. They had a couple of days to enjoy the city before any of the wedding activities.

Melody managed to work closely with Priyanka but not without scattered emotions. She kept thinking to herself that Priyanka could not possibly be a murderer and wondered why she disappeared the way she had. At times, she felt sorry for Priyanka and came close to tears. She was even sadder when she thought of Terrance. She knew that he loved Priyanka with every vessel in his heart.

Terrance was happy that his family had made it to town and was situated and enjoying the city.

Priyanka invited Terrance's family over to their home on Wednesday for dinner. She enjoyed spending time with his mother.

"Terrance, I must admit that I was a little worried when I first met Priyanka."

"Why, is that, Mom? You know I wouldn't just marry anyone." He replied jokingly."

"I don't know what it is, but there is something different about her. She seems real. She came across as fake when you brought her to Alabama. I guess she was nervous being that it was her first time in Alabama and her firsttime meeting all of us at once. I'm proud of you, son. She seems to be a real nice girl, and she fits right in with our family. Look at her over there talking to your father. If she can get him to talk then she deserves to be in the family."

Terrance turned to look over at Priyanka and his father and at that moment he felt the same as his mother. Priyanka was relaxed and very happy. He was overjoyed knowing that Priyanka was enjoying herself.

The rehearsal dinner was scheduled for the following night. Terrance's mother helped Priyanka throughout the day to make sure that everything went as planned.

"Priyanka, you look lovely. My son did good in choosing you as his wife, and I want to thank you for making him happy."

"Thank you. I feel like I'm the lucky one. Men like Terrance don't come by too often."

"Well, we raised him well. We raised him to love himself first which has allowed him to love and respect others."

"Yes, that's Terrance for you. He would give you the shirt off his back. I will admit that I was a little upset by him going to Alabama to help out Latonja."

"Why did that upset you?"

"Well, I won't make excuses. I just didn't know better. I've learned from Terrance not to judge other people because you never know their situation."

"Terrance made a promise to his friend, so I knew that he would honor that promise. Terrance values all of his friendships. I was sick to my stomach when I heard about Charlene. Terrance told me you had a hard time coming to grips with her death. He said that you felt some responsibility."

"I did feel some responsibility because she was there with me to help me to make a decision about my honeymoon. God! What I wouldn't do to have that moment in time reversed to bring back Charlene. I only knew her for a short time, but it was long enough for me to feel like we had been friends for years. You do know that she was my maid of honor, right?"

"I believe Terrance did mention that to me, and you are a very sweet girl to have invited her. But whatever you do, never walk in life with regrets. If you had known that was going to happen to her, you would not have invited her. It's as simple as that. We don't get to choose the outcome of the events of the day; we simply walk as God has ordered. God has a plan for each of us. We have to learn to let God lead and not try to create a perfect path. Life is not perfect, Priyanka. I want you to enter this marriage completely free of any burdens you may have. Ask God to free you of them."

"What great advice. Thank you for that. I really needed it."

Priyanka wiped a tear from her eye and left to join the others.

Everyone was standing in place when Jaylan received a call on his cell phone. He looked down at the number and saw that it was a call from the private investigator. He asked to be excused for a moment. Everyone gave him a funny look because they were hungry and ready for rehearsal to be over. He decided not to take the call. The rehearsal went on for another thirty minutes before dinner started. The setting was lovely. Priyanka had left nice notes at all the tables for each person expressing her gratitude. Her statement to Jaylan and Melody read, "I hope our friendship will continue to grow and get stronger with time."

Jaylan and Melody looked at each other after reading the note. They were seated at the table with Terrance and Priyanka. Jaylan's phone rang again. He looked down to see who was calling, and it was the detective again. This time after looking down at his phone, he looked up and over at Priyanka.

"Everything ok, Jaylan? You look worried about something," remarked Priyanka.

"Yeah, what's going on with you? You're acting nervous. I'm getting married tomorrow not you. You've already been through this."

"What are you guys talking about, I'm fine. It's one of my colleagues calling.

"I hope it's not business at nine o'clock on a Friday night," replied Terrance.

"No, it's not business. Well at least I don't think it is. I better check to be sure. Please excuse me for a moment. I need to call him back to see what's up since he has called twice."

Jaylan returned to the table even more nervous. He made up an excuse that something came up at work and that he and Melody had to leave so that he could look into it. Melody looked over at him with curiosity. She didn't know what was going on, but Jaylan was certainly nervous about something and was not doing a good job of hiding it. They excused themselves and told everyone they would see them the following day.

"Who was that on the phone? You were so nervous that I'm sure Terrance and Priyanka both could see that you were lying. You are not a good liar Jaylan."

"Baby, I can't talk. You just have to trust me on this one. That was the private investigator on the phone. He asked that we come to the police station right away."

"Do we have to go tonight? This can't wait? The wedding is tomorrow."

"Baby, I don't think there is going to be a wedding. I could be wrong, but there was a sense of urgency."

Jaylan and Melody entered the almost empty police station. Jaylan asked for the detective that the private investigator told him to ask for. The detective came out and led them to a room in the back.

A tall stout man with blond and black hair and a full untamed beard walked out.

"What's going on sir? Is there a problem?" Jaylan asked.

"I think you'll know shortly."

Jaylan and Melody looked at each other still puzzled about what was so important that they had to report immediately.

The detective placed one hand on the door knob to open the door to the room where he was taking them. He stopped before he completely turned the knob and told them to be prepared for what they were about to find out.

As he opened the door, Melody and Jaylan could see there was a woman in the room but couldn't see who the woman was because her back was turned.

"Sir, what is going on? Why are we here, and who is this woman?" Jaylan asked.

"It's me, Jaylan." Charlene turned to face both Jaylan and Melody. Melody got weak at the knees and almost fell to the floor before Jaylan took her into his arms. After leading his wife to a chair, Jaylan fell back to the wall behind him.

"What is going on? Charlene, we all thought you were dead. We had a memorial for you and everything. What is going on? Why haven't you been in contact with anyone?"

"Jaylan, I'm sorry. I simply did what I was told. Priyanka intentionally put her foot out causing me to fall into the woman in front of me and eventually over the rope. She wanted me dead but what she didn't know was that I'm a certified life guard. I saved the other woman. I informed the police what happened. They tried to catch Priyanka in a lie, but she was too good. They told me there was nothing that they could do. She would have gotten away with murder had I died. It was my decision to not let anyone know that I was alive because I wanted Priyanka exposed. My plan was to confront her in the ladies' room before the wedding to get her to confess. The police agreed to tape a wire to me so they could hear her confession, and that's when they were going to arrest her. I knew that Terrance would not believe that Priyanka could do something so cruel. I had to have proof even though I knew it would hurt him."

"I know how you feel, Charlene. I've been sitting on something, too." replied Jaylan.

"I know all about what you are referring to. I was called here tonight as well."

"We asked you all to come here because we have new information. We have proof to show that Priyanka is not who she says she is. We have the father of her son and her mother coming here on Monday. We are going to let her know that we know who she is and that she must tell us what happened to her son. We need to know her son is alive. And there's something else that we need you all to know. We have evidence to prove that she murdered Grant. And we are investigating another possible murder. She had a fiancé a few years ago who mysteriously committed suicide. I mean, it was believed to be a suicide."

"Wait officer, Priyanka may have done some strange things, but I can't see her as a murderer." stated Melody

"I know it's hard to imagine Melody, but she intentionally put her foot out so that I could fall over. What do you think she intended to happen? She intended to kill me. She was not comfortable about my friendship with Terrance."

"Why would she kill Grant or her fiancé? What would have been her motive?" asked Melody.

"We believe without a doubt her motive was all about hiding her true identity. Grant knew that she was Natalie. She couldn't risk him telling others. We have evidence to prove that she was there at his apartment the night he was shot. Grant had a recorder on his dining table attempting to record Priyanka for evidence. We don't know if she found out and killed him because the shooting is not on the tape, but we believe she went there with intent to kill him because she took a gun. It was his wife who discovered the recorder when she went to clear the apartment of Grant's belongings."

"We may not be able to prove she killed her first fiancé, but there's always the same possibility that he came really close to finding out who she really was," stated the private investigator who had been working with Jaylan.

"So, what's the next step? Are you guys going to arrest her tonight?"

"No, we just wanted you all to know what was going on. We won't be able to arrest her until Monday. We were not able to get a warrant for her arrest from the court due to it being late and the weekend."

"Are you saying that we have to sit and watch our friend marry a murderer?" Asked Charlene.

"That's exactly what we are saying. We don't want you all to blow this for us, and Ms.Charlene, you must stay out of site just as you have been since she attempted to kill you. We are sorry to have to ask you all to do this, but it's the only way we can keep our eyes on her until we can make a proper arrest on Monday. Is it possible for you all to come down here tomorrow morning around nine to meet with the other parties involved? We have a few other questions."

No one responded to the question.

"Well, it's late, and I know you good folks need time to think about all of this? If you can make it tomorrow morning that would be fine, if not then we will manage."

"I guess we could, but I don't know what information we will be able to give to them. We have never heard of the baby, but, yes, we will try. Charlene, I'll take you back to where you have been hiding out and pick you up tomorrow morning."

"That won't be necessary sir. We have her covered."

"Ok then let's just all go home to get some rest and pick up where we left off tomorrow morning," replied Melody.

Priyanka was not able to sleep well. She knew that something was not right. She felt that Jaylan was worried about something, and she felt he was hiding something that had to do with her. When she overhead Terrance speaking to Jaylan over the phone later that night about not being able to make it to the gym the next morning, she knew that it had something to do with her. She decided that she was going to go over to Jaylan's home early the next morning and follow him to see where he was going.

The next morning Priyanka got up as planned. She arrived at Jaylan's home around seven in the morning. She waited an hour before she saw Jaylan and Melody leave the house together.

"Why are they leaving together? Jaylan distinctly told Terrance he had to do something. Something is up and it does not feel right. God, please don't let anything interrupt my special day. Please God, let this day happen for me as I have always dreamed it would."

Priyanka followed them without their knowing. She knew something was wrong when they pulled into the police station. She didn't want to jump to any conclusions, so she parked away from the station so that they would not notice her car. She was dressed in all black with a baseball cap and tennis shoes on her feet. She got out of the car when they entered the building. She stayed close to a tree and pretended to be exercising as she watched the building. She waited and waited until she spotted Jaylan, Melody and a few other people walking out of the building together. They all stopped to talk a bit more before going to their cars. Priyanka moved a little closer to see who the other people were. It was then that she knew her life was about to take a turn for the worst. Her worst nightmare had come true. Terrance was home with his family excited about marrying her in a matter of hours while Jaylan and Melody stood there talking with her mother, Mark and Charlene of all people. She was shocked to see that Charlene had survived the fall. She didn't doubt for a minute that Charlene was there to get her arrested. She just was not sure why her mother and Mark were there but knew that Jaylan had something to do with it.

Leaning on the tree for support while still hiding, Priyanka stood staring at the group as her eyes filled with water.

"What am I going to do? Dear God, why do you have it in for me! What have I done to deserve unhappiness? This was my only chance. I'll never find love again. I can't go back to the house! I just can't! I can't go to jail!

This is not how it was supposed to happen. God, please make this go away. Please forgive me for what I have done wrong! Please! Please! Please make this go away. I didn't mean to do bad things, and I don't know where my son is! All I know is that I gave him away to a family in Maine fifteen years ago. Dear God, I made sure that I left him with a rich family. He must have had a great life! Mark has a great life! Why Lord! Why can't I have one too?"

All of these thoughts went through Priyanka's head. She finally moved when the group left and raced back to her car. She drove as calmly as she could while she collected her thoughts. She pulled over and called the airlines and made a reservation to Seattle, Washington scheduled to depart a couple of hours from the call, under the name of Leslie Osman. She went back to the house knowing that she was not going to be arrested over the weekend because she would have been arrested by now had they had the evidence needed to arrest her. She walked into her house to find Terrance still in bed. She went to her closet and pulled out her box. There within the box in a secret compartment that Jaylan overlooked were credit cards, a driver's license and passport all in the name of Leslie Osman. She sat on the floor in the closet and wrote a note to Terrance.

"Dear Terrance, I would have never imagined that I would have fallen in love with a man such as yourself; even more to have that man fall in love with me and to respect me enough to ask me to become his wife and the mother of his children. You are a kind, loving man with a family that adores you. It's ironic that I had a conversation with your mother the other day. In that conversation, she told me to live a life free of regrets. I wish that I could Terrance, but that's impossible for me. See I've done things in my life that I can't be proud of. I had a beautiful family who adored me just as much as your family adores you, but I threw them all away and treated them in a manner they did not deserve. I felt embarrassed, and I hated them for not having material possessions. I don't even know my siblings. At this very moment, the only thing that I want most now is a hug from my mother. I want to see my father's smile. I want to smell bacon cooking in that simple kitchen that my mother kept immaculate. I want to walk in the yard and plant flowers at the very house that I was embarrassed to call home. I want so much Terrance to be like you. You love your parents for who they are and not for what they have. It's funny because when we first became involved, I was angry at you for loving your past. I wanted you to forget it and walk away from it because it was a reminder of how bad I treated my family. By the time you receive this letter, you will know that I'm not the girl from Mumbai, India that I pretended to be. I'm just a simple girl from Wisconsin with a simple name of Natalie to go with it. All my life, I have for some reason believed that money was everything. I wanted to get so far away from my parents because I thought they were simple people going nowhere. I didn't want it to rub off on me. I ended up pregnant by a boy whose family had more than my family. I actually left my family and moved in with his family, but I'm sure you know this all by now. I thought they were my ticket to the American dream. In my mind, the American dream was a big house, nice car, a successful wealthy husband and a couple of children. The funny thing is that I left his family just as fast as I left my family and for all the wrong reasons. At the time, I thought they only focused on their son and his football career. I'm sure you know who he is by now too. I was so angry with that family that I left in the middle of the night with my son and never looked back. I did have a thought the other day that wherever my son is he knows his father by name and face because he's famous and known to the world, but what he does not know is that person is his father. I don't even know if the people I gave him to have told him that they are not his true biological parents. I left it up to them. They don't know who I am, and all I know about them is that they lived in Maine when I left him. It all sounds horrible, but when I left my son, I never looked back. I know with all of this information your heart will ache as it never has before, and I'm so sorry for that. My heart aches just knowing that I've hurt you so badly. I want to take this time Terrance to tell you that I, Priyanka Depesh, do take you for my husband but unfortunately, I can't stand with you at the altar today. I know in my heart that I am standing with you in life. I wish you the life you deserve and please tell your mom for me that unfortunately, I can only live to regret. I love you Terrance, and I will miss what we shared. I will never forget you. I want you so badly right now, but I know I can't have you. That hurts me more than you will ever know. I am so sorry for the things that I have done, but most of all I'm sorry for breaking your heart. You are a kind man, and I'm sure you will find that special person. I know it's going to be hard, but one day maybe you'll be able to think of me and smile. I will forever be in love with you Terrance, Love, Priyanka."

After writing the letter, Priyanka put it in the drawer where Terrance kept his keys because she knew he would find it there.

Terrance looked up to see Priyanka standing over him.

"You've been out already?" he asked.

"Yes, Baby, today is our special day. I went for a run."

"Where are you going now?"

"Baby, I have a manicure and pedicure scheduled for this morning. Technically you should not even see me today, so take a good look because this is the last time you'll see me before the wedding."

Terrance smiled and got up from the bed, hugged Priyanka and told her that he loved her. Priyanka didn't want to let go. She hugged for as long as she could without breaking down in tears.

"Go, get your manicure and pedicure, and I'll meet you at the altar," replied Terrance as he released Priyanka and watched her leave the room.

CHAPTER 36

The Wedding

S everal hours had passed and it was an hour before the wedding. The detectives and FBI were all at the wedding. They wanted to be sure to follow Terrance and Priyanka from the moment they were officially married. Terrance had been at the house all day with his family. Because Jaylan was the best man, he came to pick Terrance up to take him to the chapel. Priyanka didn't take that into consideration when she placed the letter in the drawer with his car keys. He had no idea that Priyanka was not going to make it to the wedding. He didn't think to ask about her because he knew it was against tradition. He assumed she was with Melody and the wedding planner. Once he arrived at the chapel, he could see that everyone was acting nervous.

"Terrance, I'm going to ask you a simple question that I want you to listen to carefully, ok?" cautioned his mother.

"What's going on? What's your question?"

"Melody was supposed to meet Priyanka, the wedding planner, and the other ladies at the chapel. When Melody got here, everyone was asking her if she had heard from Priyanka. They all assumed that Priyanka was with her."

"Mom, you're acting weird. What is your question?

"Have you heard from Priyanka?"

"You're kidding me, right?"

"I wish I was, but I'm not. No one has seen her today."

"I saw her this morning before she left for her manicure and pedicure," replied Terrance

"What time was that? She was supposed to meet here for those things. I've been calling her phone all day with no answer."

"You know, I never thought to call her. The groom is not supposed to have any contact. Isn't that the rule?"

"Yes son, but don't worry. I'm sure there is an explanation."

Jaylan and Melody managed to sneak away to a corner to discuss what was happening.

"She must have figured out that we were on to her. We have to tell those detectives out there that she is missing. I don't want them to think that we had anything to do with it. I think you should pull Terrance to the side and let him know as well," whispered Melody.

"You are right. We have to do it now."

Jaylan went back to Terrance and told him that he needed to speak with him. Terrance's mother asked if everything was all right. Jaylan reluctantly responded, "no."

"Terrance, I can do this in front of everyone, or you and I can speak privately."

"Jaylan, please let me know what's going on. Everyone in here is family, so it's all right to just say it."

"Man, I'm sorry. I wanted to tell you for a couple of weeks, but I couldn't. My hands were tied."

"Tell me what Jaylan?"

"There's no easy way to say this, so I'm just going to say it. Priyanka is not who she says she is. She has done some really bad things that I won't go into, but there are some detectives out there who will explain everything to you. Melody went to let them know that Priyanka didn't show up."

"Wait, you mean to tell me that detectives are out there at my wedding? Were they going to let me marry Priyanka and then take her away in hand cuffs?"

"I know, Terrance, it's seems heartless. It was the only way to make sure she stayed around. They were going to arrest her then. There is so much man that I don't know where to start, but they will explain everything to you. This hurts me as much as it does you man."

"This is unreal. I feel like I'm in a dream. You are telling me that Priyanka is a criminal? My Priyanka? My heart? I don't buy it! There has to be more to the story. Priyanka is my life and we have to find her. You all must have scared her away!"

Terrance tried to leave the room. The people in the audience could hear the commotion coming from the back but didn't know what to make of it.

"Terrance, Baby, calm down. Let's wait for the detectives to get in here so we will know the whole story. As a matter of fact, let's all have a seat and stay quiet until the detective explains it all to us." counseled Terrance's mother.

Melody called Charlene and explained everything to her and asked her to come down to the chapel. She was sure that Charlene's presence would put things into perspective for Terrance.

The detectives explained everything to Terrance. Terrance insisted that they were mistaken until Charlene walked into the room. He stood stiff not knowing what to say or do.

"It's true, Terrance. Priyanka tried to kill me, and she did all the other bad things too. It hurts but you have to understand that we have no reason to lie to you and no reason to want you to hurt. We all know how much you love Priyanka. Jaylan has been sick over this, but he had to do what he was told to do by those detectives and the FBI. We are not saying that Priyanka was a bad person with you. She is just not who we thought she was. I worry about her hurting someone else. She has proven to be capable of harming others. I can't say enough that I'm sorry, but I'm glad that I'm still alive to tell what she did to me."

Terrance didn't say another word in support of Priyanka. He simply didn't mention her name. He hugged Charlene and told her that he was glad that she was alive He walked over to Jaylan and asked him to drive him back to his house.

Melody made an announcement in the chapel that the wedding had been canceled. She apologized without explanation to people as they left the chapel.

CHAPTER 37

Leslie

Priyanka checked into the hotel under her new name of Leslie Osman after leaving her car at the train station. She was at the hotel for one hour where she colored her hair a blondish-brown color. She changed the way she would normally dress by dressing as a younger woman in hip-hop styled clothing. Standing with confidence as she looked in the mirror one last time, she smiled and left the room.

She commanded attention as she walked through the airport looking straight ahead to her destination. She pretended to be reading a magazine as she waited for her plane to board to avoid eye contact with anyone. She entered the terminal headed for Seattle. Though she entered the terminals with a lump in her throat, she never looked back.

CHAPTER 38

The Letter

Terrance barely spoke to anyone when he got home. Everyone was sensitive and tried to offer words of encouragement. Charlene decided to leave to return to her aunt to let her know what was going on and that she was alive. She decided that she was going to wait at least a month before she contacted Terrance, to give him some time. In a small way, she felt the sight of her would only be a reminder to Terrance that Priyanka tried to kill her. She didn't want him to feel any responsibility.

Jaylan and Melody stayed with Terrance for moral support. Terrance went to his room to change clothes. He reached for the drawer that held his car keys and other small belongings. As he opened the drawer to place his cuff links in the drawer he noticed a sheet of paper. The moment that he saw Priyanka's handwriting, he knew it was a note from her. He picked the note up and walked over to the bed he had shared with Priyanka. He sat on the edge of the bed and read the note. His eyes filled with tears until they overflowed and begin to fall to the page as he read the words that were tearing his heart apart. He dropped the note to the floor when he read the words "forever in love." He sat without movement because although he knew all the bad things that she had done, all he wanted to do was to hold her and to comfort her. He looked down at the note on the floor one last time and saw those words again "forever in love." He felt that no one could touch his heart as Priyanka had and for that reason he too felt as though he would forever love Priyanka.

THE END

More About The Book

"One Who Is Loved" focuses on one of the characters in the previous book "Missing Picture" This will tell the whole story of who he becomes and the challenges he faces in his professional and personal life.

More About The Author

She is a graduate of both Tuskegee University and The University of Alabama Birmingham where she earned a Bachelor of Science degree in Accounting and an MBA degree respectively. Currently working as a Lead Accountant for one of America's leading Telecommunication Corporations. She enjoys writing and volunteering her time with several charitable organizations throughout Atlanta.